A WORD THRICE UTTERED

STORIES ON LIFE'S REALITIES

PARVEEN TALHA

olive turtle

NIYOGI BOOKS

Published by
NIYOGI BOOKS
Block D, Building No. 77,
Okhla Industrial Area, Phase-I,
New Delhi-110 020, INDIA
Tel: 91-11-26816301, 26818960
Email: niyogibooks@gmail.com
Website: www.niyogibooksindia.com

Editor: Gita Rajan
Cover design: Misha Oberoi
Layout: Shashi Bhushan Prasad

ISBN: 978-93-85285-87-5
Publication: 2017

This is a work of fiction. The names, characters and incidents portrayed in it are the work of the author's imagination. Any resemblance to actual persons, living or dead, events or localities, is entirely coincidental.

Printed at: Niyogi Offset Pvt. Ltd., New Delhi, India

I dedicate this book to the memory of my dear brother Osama Talha,

Journalist, who died very young, but who lived long enough to prove

to the World that fearlessness and truth makes the pen powerful.

Contents

Preface

I find stories everywhere around me, as I have said in my earlier book. And I cannot keep them to myself. I want to share them, those observations, sketched on the canvas of my mind, refusing to be erased, left behind at times unknown, by both humans and animals. So here I am, again, ready with a collection of stories woven around facts I have observed over the years.

My earlier collection of short stories *Fida-e-Lucknow* (published by Niyogi Books) had the citizens of Lucknow as the protagonists. For it was they who had created, over time, a culture which gave Lucknow a legendary character. Through those stories the real character of the Lucknow-wala was revealed, for he had more to himself than just the hyperbole in his language; his days were not ruled by cockfights or nights by *tawaifs*. He played exemplary roles, in the two wars of Independence, during floods and droughts and during the horrible days of the Partition which played havoc with his emotions. It had separated his dear ones from him and with them had gone his property too. After the annexation of Awadh and in the in the Post-mutiny and post-Zamindari period, he found himself reduced to penury and yet did not lose his poise and dignity or self-respect. *Fida-e-Lucknow* introduced us not only to the beauty of romantic love but also unveiled the personalities of some highly empowered women from Lucknow.

And now when I browse through the stories of the present collection, I realise that the characters in most of the stories are from Lucknow again, but the canvas has expanded and spread over time and space, introducing the reader to a variety of dimensions and not just a single view. The readers' gaze is not limited to one direction. There are profiles and profiles and many angles from which he can look at the protagonist to assess for himself his or her persona.

The characters in this collection have walked through time and shown their willingness and ability to adjust to the demands of a culture which has not merely evolved but acquired an altogether new face. They have shifted to Metros and foreign capitals, faced challenges and difficult times, made success of their lives or lived patiently through failures.

My stories are not only about good men and women. Cruelty and greed rules the minds of some who make life impossible for those dealing or living with them, like the two husbands of Kausar in 'A Word Thrice Uttered'. One, a downright fraud, the other cruelty personified, one using his right to Talaq to get rid of her and their retarded son; and the other keeping his right intact as ammunition to threaten her into submission and slavery. There is the cruel wife of Masterji who has made it her life's motive to 'teach little Ram Khilawan a lesson' in 'Gangaji Is Not Far Bappa'. Manorama's husband and her three sons in 'Amma Come Back', Chaudhry the tea vendor in 'Trial and Punishment', and the Proprietor and Manager of the shoe exporting company, to which Hafizji was supplying his wares, in 'Let Sleeping Dogs Lie' are all negative characters.

In the story 'Let Me Have a Love Affair' there is this young man who is desperate to know what it is to have a love affair. That's Prashant. All he does is to concentrate on making plans and strategies to attract a girl, make her fall for him, as though he is on a shikar. He proposes and discusses marriage with her when, all the while, he is married and the father of a four-year-old child. Not once does he pause to think of the consequences, from the point of view of the girl. No doubt the girl is shattered when she discovers the facts. But she throws him out of her life and moves on. Then there is in 'Thanks For Ditching Me' a similar irresponsible young man, Imran, who had walked away from a girl's life without so much as an 'Excuse me'! But the girl, who makes a fantastic success of her life and also gets married to a good and successful man, rightly ticks him off by thanking him for ditching her, for if he hadn't, she would never have reached that pinnacle of success and happiness. It was in a fairly advanced age, discovering about her high status, that the man had dared to reach her with the excuse to 'apologise' for what he had done.

Talking about the black characters I have here touched upon two love stories that failed. But this is my way of women empowerment, warning and educating through the art of storytelling.

It is difficult at this juncture not to mention a love story which had no black characters. Love which did not sour though it did not end in marriage. That is the 'The Magic Wand', the unusual but refreshing story of a woman who admits that she had, as a young girl, been swept off her feet by a boy. There are similar indications from the boy's side too, but no expressions of love from either of them. Perhaps, because, for some reason, both had felt that their lives could only run like parallel lines, that there were no chances of them ever meeting. That could have been the reason for there being no demands and no expectations and only restraint ruling their lives. The magic which surrounded her universe in her youth keeps her spellbound at every subsequent meeting and even when they meet, when they are much older, forty-six years later.

Among the good characters Panditayin, Hafizji and Ram Khilawan and his entire family stand out most prominently. Begum Ilahi Bukhsh, Ghausia's mother, Christopher, Akbari, Aslam's father Fazlur Rehman and his grandmother will also endear themselves to the readers.

The collection does not only have black and white characters; there are grey ones too like Masterji's mother in 'Gangaji Is Not Far, Bappa,' Aunty Manorama in 'Amma Come Back', Amina, Kausar's stepmother, in 'A Word Thrice Uttered'. Marian Barret's, (Christopher's mother) character, too, certainly had shades of grey, in 'A String of Bela flowers'.

So far I have touched upon the variety of colours that paint the characters of my stories. But these do not define the stories nor can they put them in groups either, for every story carries characters of an array of shades to have a touch of reality in them. A story will be near life only if it moves with good people and bad and with those who have no particular colour, or who keep changing colour in different situations, not always because they are bad people, but because the exigencies of the situation demand that.

But it is not that these stories cannot be categorised; of course they can be, and that's one way I can touch upon them to open my mind to my readers, though I want to leave them free to interpret the stories the way they want to. Let me start with the women oriented stories with 'Virginity Lost'. I could call them women empowerment stories too. Virginity is as sacred as a deity, something to be protected and cared for and respected, but by only half the population of the world, that is women. Not only is the other half exempted, but it has the sole and exclusive right to question, put on trial and punish those who 'lose' it, though a woman can never 'lose' virginity unless man lends a helping hand! And man of course has no virginity to lose! In the story Kumkum gets convinced about these double standards and only then survives her ordeal.

'Thanks For Ditching Me,' and 'Let Me Have a Love Affair' have already been discussed in the earlier paragraphs. In both the cases the young women have taken time to recover from their setbacks but had empowered themselves in no small ways. But in 'A Word thrice Uttered', empowerment comes in old age, after what can be termed a lifetime of suffering. The story brings out my firm belief that a woman can improve her lot, only if she is willing to do so and if she has the strength to take the first step. The world is not so bad, someone or the other will come up to help.

I have included a number of stories about children in this collection. I have seen them suffering not only in poor families but also in educated well off homes if they are orphans, or if their parents are living as dependents of better-off relatives. The life of Ratan is not limited to the pages of 'Amma Come Back'. Dear Readers, open your eyes; you'll come across many Ratans around you, many Irfans and Chunnus in tea shops and many Ram Khilawans working next door.

Ram Khilawan's story is more of a novelette than a short story. The intention was not only to reveal the life but the sensitivities and aspirations of a poor child and the intensity of his love for his grandmother in the perspective of his large family. I wanted to bring into focus the compulsions and pain under which a child is sent away from home to live and work with unknown people and also the fact that poverty does not take away honesty and integrity from people's character nor does it strip or divest them of self respect.

In 'Real Sacrifice' I have dared to touch upon a very sensitive point – the Baqreed sacrifice, through the thinking processes of a child's mind. Aslam, with his childlike arguments, is able to convince the adults of his family about what a sacrifice should really entail.

I associate the suffering of animals at the hands of humans even beyond the suffering levelled by them on their weaker brethren. The animals are helpless in all situations, the Emperor of the Jungle not excluded. The two stories I have included here, are about good human beings who have befriended animals.

And next come those untiring hands of the clock which never take a rest. I wouldn't mind if they didn't but so long as they left behind some beautiful things like the Ganga-Jamuni *tehzeeb*, some values like keeping a word given to another and loving each other beyond one's community and caste. Had these values and *tehzeeb* not been in full bloom when poor Hasan was left an orphan by his Muslim aristocrat parents to the care of his nanny Panditayin, would he have grown into an educated English-knowing high official? And would Panditayin have made the efforts and taken the precautions that Hasan, despite growing up as her child, remained a Muslim.

And now after those two untiring hands have taken billions of rounds of that circular contraption we have the saga of Hafizji and his descendents who have given up fighting for their rights or even waiting for the fulfilment of the promises made to them. They prefer to 'LET SLEEPING DOGS LIE'

'The Centipede' is another story, in a lighter vein, which is a result of changed times where a bride is no longer an embodiment of shyness. Today, even in cities like Lucknow, she entertains the guests to her wedding with dance numbers like an 'item girl' does in films.

And last but not the least – the supernatural. Few believe them but most like the stories, nevertheless. Lucknow abounds in them. People narrate experiences of others. No one has an experience of his own to tell. 'A string of Bela flowers' and 'Who Brought the Delicacies' are also not my experiences.

I came face to face with the professionalism of my Publishers, NIYOGI BOOKS, during *Fida-e-Lucknow*. They just took a week to decide that they would publish that collection of my short stories. And the rest followed. This time while writing for them, I was convinced that it is an objective of work for their publishing house, not to waste the author's time, perhaps it is this mission of theirs which has enabled them to achieve, not just success, but a glorious reputation. I must thank Mr Bikash Niyogi for giving, a novice like me (which I am, as a writer, even at my age!) the opportunity to see my thoughts in print. And I must thank someone else too, that is Mrs Tultul Niyogi. It was a learning experience working with her, someone who is fast with her decisions. I asked her for a particular editor, this time Ms Gita Rajan, and by return mail she allocated my book to her.

Ms Gita Rajan is one of those few people, who have the ability to walk into the spirit of the stories and into the minds of the characters. Working with her makes my pen move in the right direction! It was a pleasure to work with her.

Now it is your turn, dear readers, to say something.

Thanks for Ditching Me

Kamal Ahmad was one of the leading lawyers of the city in the pre-Independence period, but things changed thereafter. It is not easy to find a reason for the downward slide. It could be that many of his clients went away to Pakistan. A stronger reason could have been the migration of his munshi, which made a marked difference to his practice. The munshi was a smart fellow who could bring cases from the most unexpected quarters. He could convert into litigants even those humans who were most satisfied with life. But the family pulled on. Both Kamal Ahmad and his wife Safia had tremendous control on their needs and desires. All they wanted was to educate their two daughters in the best schools of the times. On that they never compromised. And God gave them the success which they worked for. Both the children did exceptionally well in their studies. That convinced Kamal Ahmad about his daughters' abilities. At a time when just a handful of women competed for the Civil Services and even less qualified for them, he took a firm decision to prepare his daughters to sit for the competitive examinations. Thereafter he left no stone unturned to encourage them towards that goal.

When his elder daughter Nayyara completed her post graduation with a First Division and a first position in the University, Kamal Ahmad said to her, 'It is time for you to start preparing for your competitive exams. At least decide on the subjects you'll take and start collecting the necessary books.'

'Abba, I'm still not of age. I have another year and a few months,' she replied.

'I don't mean immediately. You do deserve a holiday after the strenuous labour you have put in for your Masters. But after that don't let time slide away from your hands,' her father clarified and then added, when an idea suddenly struck him, 'Why don't you visit your grandparents in Pakistan with your mother, it would be a good change for both of you.'

'Oh great, Abba, but getting the visa may take long,' Nayyara was very happy with the idea.

'Not very long, I myself will go to Delhi, let me try,' Kamal Ahmad offered. It took some time but the visas came and Nayyara accompanied her mother to Pakistan. Her mother was visiting her parents after almost a decade. This visit did create a change for Nayyara, but not a good one, as her father hoped. The younger daughter Nishat who was just a year younger than Nayyara stayed back with her father. She thought it would be best to go on a holiday after her final examinations. In Pakistan Nayyara met her uncle's son Imran, a young man who had the reputation of being handsome because he was fair. He fell for her. For the one and a half months that she was there he hung around her, showered her with compliments and praises and ultimately convinced her that he loved her. When it was time for her to leave with her mother, he even proposed to her. Nayyara came back to India with happy dreams of marrying her cousin. She forgot all about her ambitions and those of her father for her. There were many things about the young man that she overlooked like the glaring fact that he had graduated from an ordinary, wayside college and did not possess the high class education and upbringing, which she did.

But luckily she did not disclose a word about Imran's proposal, or her liking for him, or the rest of it to anyone, neither her parents nor her sister. Her mother might have guessed her inclination, but she too kept quiet. That was indeed wise of her. That knowledge would have disturbed Kamal Ahmad. Luckily again, Nayyara did not sit back waiting for the proposal, but went to the University and applied for the fellowship for research which she was awarded on the basis of her Post-graduate examinations in which she had topped the University. In course of time a vacancy for Lecturer arose in her department, which was offered to her. So Nayyara got a good enough job on the basis of her hard work. She didn't have to struggle for it.

The first two months after her return were really happy for Nayyara. She got one letter after another from her cousin. And what letters! They were laden with expressions of love and longing, replete with Urdu couplets. She would read them over and over again and still not be satisfied. Her favourite pastime was to hide and read those letters. In the third month, there was no letter, much to Nayyara's dismay.

But one fine day her uncle, his son Imran and his daughter Ilmas, casually walked into their house unannounced, as though they were a next door neighbour dropping in for a casual chat. Everyone was taken by surprise, particularly Nayyara's mother, Safia, who had never been honoured with a visit by her brother in all her married life. She was dumbfounded. She wished he had given them some notice so that she could have made proper arrangements for giving them the welcome which first time visitors deserve. At that time Kamal Ahmad's practice was at a low ebb. Obviously, the surprise visit caused a lot of embarrassment and difficulty to both Safia and her husband and to their daughters too. It was also very surprising how the three of them got their visas so fast and without any hassles. But nevertheless, the hosts kept their dignity and gave their guests a warm welcome.

Safia was sure that that her brother had come there with a purpose. She knew him too well, though in the post-Partition period she hardly met him. She didn't dare to ask him the reason. She presumed that he may have taken the journey to meet her husband, to ask for Nayyara's hand for his son. She had seen her nephew's restlessness for her. Nayyara appeared quite interested too. But Safia was sure that her husband would flatly refuse the offer. She knew her husband's mind. He was not the type of father who was in any hurry to get his daughters married. He wanted them to develop their careers with a free mind before they chose their life partners. But of course he had no idea about Nayyara's inclination.

Time unfolded that Safia was thinking far ahead of what was necessary. In another twenty days or so, the hosts realised that the guests were ready to return to their country. Till the end there was no hint of any proposal or promises thereof. And the guests left, leaving everyone in a state of surprise, and Nayyara in a state of shock. While he was there Safia's brother would often sit with her and talk to her of times gone by, about their childhood and their youth. One day he said to her, 'Safia I remember Kamal was doing very well when we arranged your marriage with him. His legal practice was flourishing.'

'Hm,' Safia agreed.

'Then what happened?' He probed.

'What can I say? Prosperity changes its course at times.'

'Things must be very difficult for you, my dear Safia,' he said with sympathy.

'Bhaijan, I am very satisfied. In fact I am happy with the way things are moving. My husband has the right priorities and we think alike, that makes all the difference.'

'But you have two daughters remember,' her brother remarked candidly.

'So what? We wanted to give them the best education and prepare them for good careers. In that, with God's grace, we've been successful. The rest is in Allah's hands.' Safia said that with a kind of finality. Her brother must have sensed that Safia did not want further discussions on the topic. So he decided to put a full stop with a compliment, 'How happy you have made me Safia, with the way you run your home and give respect and dignity to your husband.'

That conversation with her brother left a deep impression on Safia's mind. She became convinced that since there had not been much interaction between the families except through letters, ever since the Partition, her brother wanted to examine for himself everything about the present condition of her family—the finances, the friends, the movements of the girls.

While they were there, Imran expressed as much fondness for Nayyara as he had done in his own home, though Nayyara was inhibited. Perhaps, with her father around, she could not but remain reserved.

On his return Imran wrote just one letter to her. After that there was a big gap. That was also the time when Indo-Pak skirmishes were being reported from the Kutch border. Just before the war started and the postal system between the two countries snapped, Nayyara got one more letter in which the expressions of love were not as profuse as in the earlier ones. There was a certain lack of warmth in the last letter. After that the postal system remained suspended for the next six months. That was a traumatic period for Nayyara. She tried all kinds of ways to reach Imran through the post via relatives settled in other countries. But she received no reply from him, which convinced her that her letters were not reaching him. And yet she remained confident that he was also trying to be in touch with her through the means available to him.

At last when the postal services were reopened she tried writing directly to him. After a few months she did get a letter from him which, surprisingly, was full of rebukes and criticism directed more at her family, particularly her mother and sister. He chided her for sending him letters through 'all sorts of people.' He told her that her mother and sister were very arrogant and 'he is ashamed to have relatives like them.' Another letter came to her from Imran's younger sister, Ilmas. She wrote to her to refrain from writing to her brother because he had got engaged to a very beautiful girl. 'Her father is a very high Police Officer, who is getting him a good job in the National Airlines,' she informed. She also advised, 'Look Nayyara there is no comparison between Bhaiyya and you. He is so handsome and you are dark. Don't dream of the impossible.' For Nayyara it was the end of the world. She found it impossible to understand how things could have changed to that extent in the six months after Imran and his family visited India. As far as she could recall he went back quite pleased with everything. He even sent two letters to her after reaching home, one of which was definitely overflowing with love. The other one was also not all that bad.

Nayyara was shattered but she did not reveal her condition to anyone, neither at home nor to her friends. She was particularly careful that her parents and sister were kept ignorant about the insulting letters that she received from Imran and his sister. If the facts in the letters had reached her mother she would definitely have complained to her brother and her mother about the disgrace levelled at her and her daughters. That would have made the matter public and embarrassed her more. She decided to bear the pain and keep everything to herself. She started spending more time at the University so that people at home did not notice her trauma for if they did she would be in a fix. They would definitely question her. She did not want that.

But she did not compromise with her self-respect and dignity despite the unexplainable insults levelled at her and her family by someone who had become the focus of her emotions. She took a decision not to write to him again. And she did not. Ignoring him and his relatives was a good decision. That helped her to move on. Though rebuilding her self-confidence took some time and delayed her preparation for the Civil Services exam, which her father was keen on and which had also been her dream at one time. She could not concentrate on her preparation. Finally she told her father that she was not sufficiently prepared and that she would take her chance the next year.

'Next year would be your last chance; you will be over-age after that, my child. Supposing you miss appearing in that examination for some reason. One doesn't know what may happen tomorrow. Or you may not qualify. You will never forgive yourself for not taking the two chances available to you,' her father said, despair ringing through his voice.

'Abba, isn't the University job good enough?' she queried.

'No! Definitely not. You'll realise that later in life. Besides the job is temporary. When the permanent lecturer comes back from abroad you'll have to hand it back to him,' he explained.

'I'll be considered for the next vacancy. And what is the point of appearing this year when I know I will not be successful,' she persisted.

'Look my child, there are full five months left. And there is still time for sending the forms. Don't be negative. If you study with full concentration there is nothing that can stop you,' her father almost begged. But she walked away without a word.

She entered her room and sobbed herself to sleep. But she found herself wide awake in the middle of the night. After that, sleep distanced itself from her, and so did peace. Her father's disappointed face kept appearing before her with sadness oozing out of his eyes. Suddenly she sat up on her bed and said to herself, 'How broken I am because a man I knew for just a month and a half has let me down. Haven't I done the same to my loving father?' The next minute she decided not to let go her chance that year. She realised that her father's advice was for her good.

As the first ray of sunlight entered her room she rushed out and went to her father. He was spreading his prayer mat for his Fajir Namaz. Surprised to see Nayyara at that hour he asked, 'What is the matter Nayyara?'

'Abba, I'll appear for the exams this year. I'll sit with you after breakfast and fill up the forms.'

'A very good decision, by a very wise girl! I'll see you after the Namaz,' he put his hand lovingly on her head. His face betrayed that he too had not slept the whole night.

From that moment on, all her focus was on the examinations. It was not easy. The Imran episode would keep coming back, at times saddening her, at times irritating her. But she soon reasoned out that it was not love they shared. He just wanted some fun. It was no love on her part either. It was her ego that was shattered when he dropped her like a hot brick. She tried to convince herself that he decided against her not because there was anything wrong with her, but because she was more educated than him and because her parents' financial position had weakened. And this reasoning pushed her towards greater hard work. She started realising that the time had come for her to stand by her father, to raise the status of the family.

And that helped. She was able to prepare, for the examination, to her satisfaction. And finally she did well. The results were better than her expectations. She was chosen for the Diplomatic Services because she was ranked very high on the merit list. The status of the family, of course, shot up overnight. But more than that was the breeze of joy that touched everyone's heart, particularly her father's. For Nayyara it was the ultimate. There was not a moment in her life, thereafter, when she didn't find, some occasion, to thank God for having given her a father like her 'Abba.'

But she had still not been able to stop her mind from thinking about Imran. He would step in, at times, into her mind and knock, causing anger and irritation. Then a time came when the thought of Imran would embarrass her. She started feeling ashamed of that episode. She would curse herself for having wasted almost two precious years of her life for a personality so insignificant, for a human so heartless. And the time did come; the time did not take long in coming, when the Imran incident was wiped out from her mind. She became indifferent to him altogether.

While she was still a probationer, she met Riyasat from her own service. They fell in love and got married. Both their families approved and were happy. In the meanwhile her job took her from one promotion to another, from one honour to a greater one. She faced challenges and got recognition.

Almost at the end of her career, when she was posted as the topmost diplomat in a foreign country, her Private Secretary informed her that a person who introduced himself as her first cousin and gave his name as Imran Husain had been calling for several weeks to get an appointment from her.

'I did not inform you earlier because you were out of the country. And Madam, today he has already reached the office and is waiting outside the office building.' Nayyara was indeed surprised, but without lifting her eyes from her work, she told her Private Secretary, 'Right now I am busy, as you can see. If he can come in the afternoon, call him at 3:30.'

At 3:30 a haggard old man walked nervously into her office. If she had seen him without knowing who he was she would never have recognised him. But she smiled at him and asked him as to what brought him there. He told her that that he lived in that country after migrating from his own. He was almost wriggling in his chair, with embarrassment, but he still managed to say that he had come to apologise for all that had happened. 'Because I went back on my word, you decided to remain unmarried. It is your maiden name on the board outside,' he said, sympathy oozing out of his voice.

Nayyara's smile became broader. 'Actually *I should have come to you,* to thank you for ditching me. Could I have reached this position, had I, God forbid, married you? And could I have then got a husband, as honest and affectionate and of a high status as my husband Riyasat?' Imran's face drained of whatever blood there was in his veins. She added, 'And let me inform you. A modern married woman doesn't change her name. She has a right to her own name.' Looking pointedly at the clock on the wall she said, 'Thank you for your visit,' and calmly resumed her work, without once looking up at Imran, staggering out of her office.

Rustam

My father purchased a one-horse carriage in the year 1947, from an army officer who had opted for Pakistan. The transaction cost him ₹ 300/ only, though Rustam, the horse and the stately carriage was worth much more. Muslim property was going at incredibly low prices in those troubled times. Those who had decided to make their homes in the new country were in a hurry to dispose off their property at any price and leave. But there was another reason in this case. The seller family refused to take a price for Rustam.

Major Ilahi Bukhsh, the army officer, had already left Lucknow for Rawalpindi. His wife had stayed behind with her two daughters, since both the girls had to appear for their high school examination in March. It was she who completed the transaction before leaving.

'Rustam is our child, we cannot sell him.' The touching farewell of the family with Rustam, which followed, brought our two families together. Before that we were total strangers.

'The army is so well equipped, can they do nothing to transport their officers' livestock till Rawalpindi, Begum Sahiba?' my father asked.

'Sir, the decision to leave Rustam behind came only after we tried our best to get him transported to Pakistan and failed. There is just no way out.'

'Begum Sahiba, you still have two weeks before you leave. Keep Rustam with you till then. May I also try to find a way out?' my father insisted.

'Sir you are very kind. Go ahead, maybe Allah intends to help us through your auspicious efforts,' Begum Ilahi Bukhsh said, her heart full of hope.

My father's efforts also failed. He should have known that the subcontinent was burning. There was hatred all around. Those were not the times for emotions. People were forced, in many places in the Punjab, to leave behind even their children or old parents, if they were not able to keep pace with the group they were walking with, towards, what they thought, would be their new homes.

When it was time for them to leave for Pakistan, Begum Ilahi Bukhsh and the two girls came themselves to our house in the carriage to leave behind Rustam. That was the only way to do it. Rustam had refused to budge from their house, with our coachwan driving the carriage. Another heartbreaking scene followed.

'I am taking my two daughters with me but I am leaving my son with you,' Begum Ilahi Bukhsh said, to my parents, and then went on to explain how Rustam's mother, who pulled their carriage before him, died when Rustam was born and how she, her husband and her two daughters kept him in their bedroom and bottle-fed him till he could eat on his own. Even thereafter Rustam spent all his free time in the veranda adjacent to their bedroom. He would peep in through the window and play pranks. My parents and other relatives, who were themselves in tears, assured her that all possible care would be taken of the horse.

'But Begum Sahiba,' my father said, 'even if we treat him better than you did, it appears to me, that for Rustam, we will never be able to replace you and your family.' He was right. We never could. With all our love and care, we could do nothing to erase the pain of separation from his heart. For two years Rustam would run with the carriage, each time he was harnessed to it, head straight for the Cantonment and stop only at the house in Dilkusha, where he lived with his earlier masters. The new incumbents kept their gate locked. But Rustam would not give up. He'd try to force his way into the house till he was fagged out. Our coachwan would patiently wait till a disappointed Rustam was willing to come back with him.

Nor did he like his new masters to sit in the carriage. The moment anyone entered the carriage, he would stand on his hind legs and turn the vehicle vertical, with people inside screaming for life.

All this while, my parents remained in regular correspondence with Major and Begum Ilahi Bukhsh. They were bound by a promise made to Begum Sahiba that they would keep her informed about Rustam's *khairiat*, his well being through a postcard. In the beginning the letters from Pakistan were desperate enquiries about Rustam and pleas made to my parents to look after his wellbeing. They would almost beg them not to treat Rustam like a beast of burden. They would list the things he should be given to eat and those he should never ever eat. Gradually the letters became less desperate but the gap between them never increased. The correspondence never stopped. Letters of enquiry about Rustam's wellbeing kept pouring into our home regularly.

Even Eid, Baqreed and New Year greetings never came without enquiries about Rustam, though the couple always wrote that they were convinced that Rustam was in safe hands.

It took, indeed a long time, but Rustam finally gave up and became somewhat obedient to our coachwan, or maybe the coachwan learnt to rein him. Rustam stopped heading for his earlier home, as he did for two long years. And much to everyone's relief he also stopped standing on his hind legs with people sitting inside the carriage. Rustam had no doubt become very duty conscious and amiable, perhaps loyal too. But my father was convinced that he was not happy and that he was still missing his original family.

'What makes you think that Rustam is not happy, how are you so sure?' My mother asked.

'I have had a glimpse of him when he was with the Ilahi Bukhsh family and was ignorant of his impending separation.' My father said and then he described the scene he witnessed the first time he visited Major Ilahi Bukhsh's house to enquire about the one-horse carriage which the family wanted to sell. When he stepped into the house he found Begum Sahiba sitting on a bench in the lawn and Rustam jumping and running around. He would run up to her and shove his head into her stomach. She'd shout at him with mock anger and give him a gentle push. He'd run back to her and rub his face on her sari. It was in the midst of such happy activity that father introduced himself and told her what he had come for. Begum Sahiba got up with a start, her face drained of all colour. She appeared to have woken up from a very pleasant dream to the nightmarish reality of having to take the most unpleasant decision of her life, a decision, which she could not postpone. Rustam continued to run around. He ran again towards Begum Sahiba and shoved his face on to her stomach like before. This time Begum Ilahi Bukhsh kissed his forehead and clutched on to him and started weeping. Her two daughters also put their faces on his back and cried bitterly. Rustam forgot his pranks. He sat down on the floor, put his chin on the begum's lap and gave out a wail more painful than all the tears of the three women put together.

'Such moments of intimacy which Rustam shared with Begum Ilahi Bukhsh, I have only seen between a human child and his mother,' my father said and after a pause added, 'in this house Rustam has never played like that with anyone.'

'But he no longer stands on his hind legs nor does he run to his Dilkusha home anymore, I think he has started liking his life here now,' my mother insisted.

'He doesn't go to his old house in Dilkusha anymore because he sees no reason to go there. He went there every day for two long years, but never found a single known face in the house. He was not allowed in; the gates were closed on him. And since he doesn't understand the compulsions of the Partition, he could be feeling betrayed and abandoned by the people he loved so much. And if you think he has become obedient, what else could he have done. Had he any options? Had he any other choice?' my father asked.

'Come on, you talk as though animals live by emotions as humans do.' My mother said in a lighter vein.

'For some animals emotions do play a strong role though the role of instincts in their activities cannot be ruled out altogether,' father explained.

Rustam occupied the thoughts of everyone in our family. We could only hope he was happy and adjusted to his new surroundings but deep within we knew that the pain of separation from the Ilahi Bukhsh family still lingered in his heart.

Surprisingly after the Eid of 1953 there was no letter from the Ilahi Bukhsh family. Our greetings at Baqreed and New Year also remained unanswered. Then one day, at the end of January, while working in his chamber, my father heard Rustam neighing in a peculiar manner. The sound, he thought, was very strange, so he rushed out and went straight into the veranda where Rustam lived. But he was not there. My father found him standing in the courtyard looking at the sky and neighing. Hearing my father's footsteps he rushed towards him and did something which he had never done before. He put his chin on father's shoulders and let out a wail, no less painful than the one he had heard on his first visit to the Ilahi Bukhsh house. Before father could react Rustam rushed towards the door. In a jiffy he was out on the road and before anyone could run after him, he was out of sight.

Father and the coachwan decided to rush to the house where Major Ilahi Bukhsh lived with his family, though Rustam had not gone there for the last four years. Without wasting anytime they hired a rickshaw and left for the Cantonment. They thought they would catch up with him on the way. But Rustam could not be sighted. When they reached the house in Dilkusha they found the gate wide open and a kindly old Sardarji standing near it.

'Looking for your horse?' As soon as my father lighted from the rickshaw, Sardarji asked with a smile.

'Yes, Bhai Sahib, but we have never seen you here before?'

'I was Major Ilahi Bukhsh's neighbour when Rustam was born. I saw all those happy years of the family with him. He was the apple of their eyes. When they left for Pakistan, I was in Poona. I was transferred there. The house is now allotted to my son who is also in the army. I live with him now that I have retired. Your horse is inside,' Sardarji said and asked my father and the coachwan to follow him. They found Rustam running up and down the veranda behind the master bedroom. It was in that veranda that Rustam used to live and play pranks with Begum Ilahi Bukhsh, during happier times. Rustam spent more than an hour walking around the house expecting to find someone, while father sat, patiently on a chair, waiting for him.

At last he came to my father, put his chin on his shoulder and let out a heart- rending wail once again. Father kissed him on his forehead and hugged him like Begum Ilahi Bukhsh had done on that fateful day, so long ago. The next minute Rustam moved his face from father's shoulder to his knee where he rested his chin just for a split second and then kind of slipped away gently on the ground. Father bent down to caress him. But Rustam did not respond. He was no longer in this world.

When father returned home with Rustam's body, there was a telegram waiting for him from Kubra in Pakistan:

'MOTHER PASSED AWAY THIS MORNING' ... KUBRA

Kubra was Begum Ilahi Bukhsh's daughter.

Amma! Come Back......

Ratan had nothing in his heart against his mother, for keeping him away from her for almost all his childhood years, though he spent them in extreme misery. He understood that his mother had to spend those years trying to earn some money for his future, the best way she could. She belonged to a very educated family, he knew that, but was quite weak in studies herself. She sat twice for the high school examinations and failed. Her family was not doing well financially. Her brother was without a job for many years. He had tried his hand at several business ventures, which also brought no success. With her level of qualifications, Sudha was not likely to get a respectable job, within the country. Even the Gram Sevika's job which she held in the 1950s raised some eyebrows. On the contrary if she went abroad and served a family there, friends and relatives would not know what exactly she was doing and she would come back with an amount which would help her and her son to live well.

Ratan knew that was the reason why his mother consented to go abroad to work with diplomats' families after her marriage failed, leaving him under her sister's care. She did that out of sheer helplessness. Those couldn't have been happy years for her either. He never held his mother guilty for all that he suffered. That was his destiny he believed. But he prayed all his life, even as an adult, that no other child be left without parents. That was a tall order, even for God, to fulfil. Ratan knew that. So Ratan decided not to have children. He was paranoid. He felt that if he did, despite his intentions, their destiny would not be in his hands; just as Sudha's destiny was neither in her mother's hands, nor his in Sudha's hands.

Sudha's mother consented to her marriage with the rich widower living in faraway Bengaluru, because she thought it was a good option for her. She wanted Sudha to live in comfort. The man did give her a comfortable life but for just a few months. Gradually, Sudha came to know that her husband was not normal. His abnormality increased with time. She noticed that though he was alright during the day and treated her well, as evening approached, he'd start behaving strangely. And after taking a few pegs, he would become violent. He was not recognisable by night. Even his violence Sudha tolerated for some time, but then he had started burning her with cigarette ends and even with lighted candles. For Sudha the setting of the sun meant the opening of a torture cell. When she could bear no more she wrote to Manorama, her eldest sister, all about her suffering. It was Manorama's husband who had arranged her marriage to the old man.

Sudha was quite happy working as a Gram Sevika in a village very close to her home in Lucknow. Her salary, though meagre, gave her great satisfaction. And she felt quite secure too because her mother stayed with her. It was her misfortune that her brother-in-law came across the old business man in

Bengaluru who wanted to get married. And he was successful in convincing Sudha's mother, who had, till then, found no other better alliance for her.

Sudha's letter to her sister brought no relief for her. In her reply the sister wrote a long letter full of advice, asking her to pull on somehow and explained that it was not her husband's fault. His intentions were good. He obviously knew nothing about those terrible traits of the man. Sudha was pregnant and could take the torture no more. She packed a small suitcase, bought a train ticket to Lucknow and went back to her mother, where she stayed on. Despite her mother's persuasion, Sudha refused to go back to her husband. It was at Lucknow that her son, Ratan, was born. After a few years her eldest sister Manorama took her and her son to her home in Delhi. Sudha had all intentions of returning to her mother in Lucknow after a few months. But after sometime the sister's husband came up with a suggestion.

'Sudha, I have very a good job for you in mind,' he said.

'What sort of a job can I get? I have not even passed the tenth class. Despite that, God had given me a good job, which you forced me to leave and got me married to that monster.'

'I did not force you, my dear girl. I only persuaded you with all good intentions.'

'Comes to the same thing,' Sudha said with tears in her eyes, 'If I had continued as a Gram Sevika I would have been a Block Development Officer in these last seven years, because I would have continued with my studies privately. Sooner or later I would have got a degree.'

'Yes that was my fault. I gave more importance to your marriage, because you were getting on in age,' her brother-in-law said. Surprisingly he had not lost his temper.

'Alright, now tell her what job you have in mind for her,' his wife prodded.

'Sudha, I know a Naval Attaché who is going as a diplomat to Australia with his family. I know his wife also; your sister also knows them. They keep visiting us. I will introduce you to them. You can meet them tomorrow. They need someone to look after their house in Australia. If you could go with them ...'

Before he could complete his sentence Sudha started weeping, 'You want me to be their household servant after snatching such a respectable job from me. Do you know, the people in the village, where I worked, used to touch my feet?' Sudha's brother-in-law realised that he had touched a raw nerve. He said nothing more that evening and immediately left with his wife for their room.

But the following day the Naval Attaché and his wife called on them. Sudha's sister and brother-in-law gave them a warm welcome. Sudha too must have spent a long time thinking about the offer, for surprisingly she also sat with them and participated in the conversation and finally consented to accompany them to Australia, even though she was not allowed to take her three year old child with her. Sudha was a loving mother; she must have seen something good for the child in that decision.

That was the first time when she left Ratan with her sister. He was seven when Sudha came back. On her return she realised that the Naval Attaché could have paid her a better salary though she admitted that he and his wife treated her like family. And yet she was hardly with her son for a year, when she went again and then again, each time with different diplomats and their families and to different countries. When she came back finally to be with her son he was already thirteen.

The best years of Ratan's childhood were spent waiting for her to be with him. Those were years of fear and anxiety, too long and dark for that little child to comprehend. He thought they would never end. His mother's letters, the parts which were about him or which were addressed to him, would be read out to him by his aunt when his uncle was in office. That would bring him some joy. Sometimes he would ask her to read it again. And she would willingly oblige. At times he would be full of hope that his mother would come back to him soon. At times he'd think that she would never come or would come only after a very long time. Between hope and depression life, for Ratan, just crawled on.

The only person he could dare to talk to was his aunt. He was scared of her husband, that man with a foul temper and more scared of their three sons and their long winter holidays which they spent with their parents. Life was a torture for him till they went back to their prestigious hill schools where they studied. They treated him as though he was their equal in age, though even the youngest of the three was a decade older than him. Once, when his aunt was out shopping, the eldest, who was fifteen years older than Ratan, twisted his arm, just for the fun of it. All three wanted to see how the little one would react. Knowing his cousins too well, the poor boy was petrified and fainted due to the severe pain. His tender bones could not bear the force of that strong adult hand and cracked in several places. The incident happened in the veranda outside the kitchen. Luckily Dil Bahadur, their young servant, who was in the kitchen, sensed that something had gone wrong. He rushed out, picked up the child and ran to the government dispensary which was not far. The boy did recover. Even his bones were set in place, after a couple of months in plaster, thanks to Dil Bahadur and the competent orthopaedic surgeon, who was on duty in the dispensary at that time. But the child was traumatised for life. This was an unbearable physical pain which was inflicted on Ratan at a very young age. But something worse than this physical pain was waiting for him.

The couple had a house in a village like small town, which was a few hours from Delhi, where they settled down after their retirement. They were hardly there for a year when they were allotted the plot of land which they had booked in Delhi. Now they wanted to build a house on that land. Both of them went back to Delhi to supervise the construction, leaving nine-year-old Ratan to look after the village house along with the gardener. For Ratan life couldn't get worse. The day would pass somehow, thanks to a roadside school in which his uncle had admitted him, but the nights were too scary to bring him any sleep. Even in that frightening atmosphere simple little Ratan never dared to imagine that he could run away. It was during those long nights that he found solace in praying to God, asking Him to tell his mother to put him in the care of his Lucknow Aunt Shakuntala. He had visited her twice with his aunt Manorama. Shakuntala he thought was the best person he had ever met. She really loved him. Once when he was with his Aunt Shakuntala on his birthday, she actually bought a cake and cold drinks, made chaat and sweets, and called guests to celebrate his birthday. He had never cut a cake before, never got presents either. The memory of that event made him so happy. He thought he should write a letter to his mother telling her to send him to his Aunt Shakuntala. He wrote many letters and tore up each one, because he thought his writing was not good enough nor his spellings. He also did not know her address. And he never dared to ask anyone else to help. There was only the gardener around. And he would not know his mother's address, he thought.

It was during those long frightening months that he was reminded of the chocolates his mother would send through diplomatic bags with the help of her boss. He'd never get more than four small pieces each time they were sent. The rest would be gobbled, right away, by his cousins. But the worst was when his favourite toy, a gun was sent to him. He had gone once with his mother to Khan Market when she was in Delhi, just about to leave for her second assignment. He saw a very expensive toy gun which he wanted to buy. His mother told him that she would get a better one in the foreign country she was going to. She would send it immediately. The boy created no fuss. He accepted readily as he always would. The mother kept her promise. The toy gun came in a diplomatic bag in no time. The aunt told him about it and took out the packet from the bag for him. As he stretched his hand for it, the uncle said, 'Manorama, are you crazy, the boy is too small to handle such an expensive toy. On Sunday is Brigadier Surjit Singh's grandson's 10th birthday. We'll give it to him. I'm the only subordinate he has invited to the party. The Brigadier will be so impressed with me, when he sees the foreign toy.' Turning to the shocked seven year old he said, 'Beta, we'll get a gun for you from Sarojini Nagar, I'll take you to the market myself, okay.'

'Okay' the little one answered with no sound coming from his lips. But any sensitive person could have heard the tears in his throat and seen his heart bleeding like a stream.

After a few months his Aunt Manorama came, with her husband, to look up if all was well in the village house. That brought a great relief for Ratan in that lonely house. But in a few days they were ready to go back. Ratan was heartbroken. As his aunt moved out of the house he held on to her sari and wept. 'Mausi take me with you, I can't live here alone.' He dared to say that much, but could say nothing more. He was hysterical. That moved Manorama. 'Come come, Ratan, I'll take you with me, don't cry.'

'What do you mean, who will look after this house?' her husband, who was standing behind her, shouted.

'Can this child look after this house or any house?' Manorama for once shouted back at her husband, and said. 'I will go only if Ratan goes back with me.'

Just then the gardener intervened, 'Sahib, I will look after the house. If you don't trust me you could lock up everything. The child is too small to live alone.'

Perhaps the gardener's intervention put a little shame and maybe some sense into the sahib's head. He sat down in the car with his wife and Ratan, after locking the house and leaving the keys with the gardener. He did not grumble as usual in the car on his way back. In fact, he tried to politely explain to his wife, why he wanted to leave Ratan behind. 'You have been so ill for the last few months, Dil Bahadur has gone away. You are hardly able to cook for the two of us, you are always tired. Glaucoma has weakened your vision too. That was the only reason why I told you not to bring Ratan.'

Even before his aunt could reply, Ratan offered, 'Mausa I can cook now, I have learned cooking from the gardener. I will also clean the house and wash the dishes. Mausi, I will do all the work that Dil Bahadur did. You can rest and have your medicines and get well.' Poor Ratan was willing to do anything to escape living alone in that big house, surrounded by jungles.

'No beta, I will manage, don't worry,' Manorama, put her hand on Ratan's head with affection. She felt guilt pricking her conscience for abandoning the child in that god forsaken house for so long. 'And for no valid reason,' she said to herself, 'I should have put my foot down before like I did now.'

But Ratan wanted to please them by whatever way he could. He didn't want a repeat of the exile. He started in all earnest. Not a single day did he miss washing the dishes and sweeping the floor as best as his little hands could. Life became convenient for Manorama, though she had to do the cooking.

One day a visitor came to their house, who saw Ratan washing the dishes. She stayed on for some time and saw him sweeping the floor too. That visitor was Aunty Shakuntala's husband's favourite niece Shrishti, who was incidentally a great friend of Ratan's mother. Shrishti was pained to see Ratan's plight. She was going back to America, where she had settled, with a stopover at London where Sudha worked. And there Shrishti met Sudha, just to tell her about the pathetic condition under which her son lived in Manorama's house. She advised her to send him to live with her sister Shakuntala, till her work at London was over.

'Shakuntala Aunty is so fond of children and so is my uncle. They have no children of their own. They'd love Ratan to be with them, and Ratan too, will be very happy there.' Shrishti explained.

And that's how Ratan's prayers to the Almighty were answered. Shakuntala, her husband and Ratan made a happy threesome. But now the problem was Ratan's education. He was almost twelve and had never attended school continuously even for a year. All those gaps were to be filled up somehow, by tuitions, coaching, extra classes and whatever else. Ratan put his soul into his studies. Within a year his mother also came back, never to take up a job again. And now Ratan was with two mothers both vying with each other to give him the best. Ratan would sometimes pinch himself to be sure that he was not dreaming.

Though his education took some extra time, as gaps caused by his earlier erratic schooling had to be filled, he did quite well in his studies. He also earned a prestigious fellowship to do post graduation in Germany. He came back immediately after his studies and never accepted a job that would take him away from his mother. All he wanted was to be with her and with Aunt Shakuntala and her husband. His only ambition was to provide for them what they needed. God gave them long lives and Ratan tried to make their lives as happy as he could. The three of them were successful in convincing him to get married, to a girl of his choice, but they failed to convince him to have children. The fear of his traumatic childhood being repeated in the life of another innocent child never left him.

A String of Bela Flowers

Christopher, his mother Marian and brother Bryan were to leave India for England in April 1962 and settle in Glasgow. Marian was from Scotland where, in the mid-1930s, she met an Indian Christian doctor and married him. The couple decided to settle in Lucknow, the hometown of the doctor. Their life in Lucknow began on a happy note. They lived in a large palatial house with manicured lawns on all sides and dozens of servants. The doctor's practice had started with a bang and showed great promise. Marian felt the world was at her feet. But when Bryan was seven years old and Christopher just six, the happy times came to a sudden end. Their father developed tuberculosis and after fighting with the disease, bravely and patiently for a year, quietly passed away into the next world.

And then began a life of struggle for Marian and her two kids. The large house they lived in was built by the doctor's father. Not long after the doctor's death his father also passed away and the house was divided between his eight children. Marian and her children were left with three small rooms at the rear end of the large house. She took up a teaching job in a convent, where the nuns gave her more affection than she expected. But making both ends meet was not easy.

And yet she never thought of returning to England because in Lucknow she had made a large circle of friends, very warm and helpful. The servants, who looked after her children when she was at school, were devoted, loyal and duty conscious. Such help, Marian was sure, she would never get anywhere in England. She stayed back in Lucknow to bring up her children. And she never regretted her decision, for her sons grew up into well mannered young gentlemen. She was able to give them the education she wanted. The elder son became a lecturer and the younger one studied medicine from King George's Medical College which was his father's alma mater.

By the mid 1950s a lot of Anglo-Indian families started moving out of Lucknow to England. Many families went to Australia too. In fact Anglo-Indians all over India were shifting their homes to England or Australia. It was then that Marian remembered England, her home till the mid 1930s. By the end of the 1950s, Marian had made up her mind to go back to England. She took the decision because the Anglo-Indian community around her had convinced her that her sons would have a better future in England.

Her brothers, whom she had left behind in Britain had given her a different advice altogether. She had herself never got an opportunity to visit her home in England during the twenty-six years that she spent in India. But she was in regular correspondence with her two brothers who lived in Glasgow. These two brothers had dinned into Marian's head, through their letters, that there was no social acceptance in the British society for the mixed lot who were coming from India. 'You are lucky, dear Marian, that neither of your sons has inherited the colour of their father's hair nor eyes nor skin. No one can doubt their pure English descent. They can pass off as Englishmen! Just ensure both of them come to England unattached. Here in England they can get married to English girls and give their children a respectable future,' one of her brothers had written to her. This advice, Marian had passed on to her sons, several times.

Bryan had no problems with the advice but Christopher had.

'Mummy, in that case why should we go to England? You have stayed in India for a quarter of a century, your children and you have been showered with respect and love. What makes you think that we will not get the same love and respect in future?' Christopher asked.

'Times are changing darling; India is not the same as it was before Independence. The future will not be the same as the past was for us. Don't forget, the Indians associate us with the British.' Marian tried her best to convince her son.

'What do you mean by *the Indians*, Mummy, aren't we Indians too?'

'Yes we are but of another colour, we speak another language, we pray at a different place of worship,' his mother said.

'In England too we will have to fake our identity to get acceptance. Doesn't Uncle Charles say so in his letter?'

'Yes he does, but that will be easy. Both of you look totally British.'

'All of us don't look British. Lynette has black hair, black eyes and a dark complexion.' Christopher reminded.

'Who is Lynette?' Marian asked with anger.

'Lynette D'Cruze, dear mother. Do I also have to tell you that she is the girl your son Christopher is going to marry before leaving for England?' There was thunder in Christopher's voice.

Lynette's mother Marjorie was a colleague of Marian in the convent. Both were kindergarten teachers. Their children had grown up together. Everyone in the two families knew how close Christopher and Lynette were to each other. For Christopher, life without Lynette and for Lynette, life without Christopher, was unthinkable. Christopher was surprised at his mother's reaction and rightly so, because Marian had never before objected to his friendship with Lynette. It was taken for granted in their two families that they will get married as soon as Christopher completed his MBBS. Was Marian so desperate now to have her sons accepted as the pure race in the British society, that she was willing to sacrifice their happiness? Both the brothers couldn't understand their mother's change of mind.

Bryan tried to reason with his mother, 'Mummy you are taking us to England for a better future. But if our very acceptance in that society depends on our being pure British why shouldn't we stay back here, and hope for the best.'

But Marian had made up her mind. The difficulties she had faced after her husband's death hadn't ended till her sons had completed their education. No one from her husband's family lent a helping hand all those years. Even Christopher realised that. He was also aware, much to his embarrassment, that his mother's difficulties had increased manifold when he expressed his desire to become a doctor like his father. But his mother, despite the limited finances at her disposal, kept a cheerful face and never once mentioned the hard work she took upon herself to earn that extra money to pay for his education. She gave tuitions at home till late evening. But what both her sons found very painful was to see her walk a couple of kilometres every day to a raja's house and back, to give tuition to his two daughters who were in strict purdah.

It was a good amount she got from him. But she still couldn't afford to take a rickshaw.

Bryan and Christopher knew, since the time they were old enough to understand, that their mother missed her home and people and still she only concentrated on their education and wellbeing. She never even thought of taking a holiday home. And they also knew that the decision she had taken then, was not because she wanted to be with her long lost family, but because she wanted to give her sons a better future. Christopher didn't mind leaving Lucknow to go to England. That sacrifice from him his mother deserved, he thought, but not without Lynette. For him all plans had Lynette at centre stage. For Christopher life without Lynette had no meaning.

He tried his best to explain that to his mother. He begged, he shouted, he threatened, but couldn't defy. After many a thunderous scene between mother and son, it was the son who gave in.

He had kept Lynette informed of his mother's change of heart, but he also kept sharing with her his hope that he would be able to convince her. He was genuinely sure he would be successful. But his efforts failed. And finally, for Christopher, his mother's sacrifices weighed heavier than his love for Lynette. Christopher finally told his mother that he was prepared to go with her to England unattached on condition that she would never ask him to get married. Marian was happy because she felt, that sooner or later, she would be able to convince him to settle down with a girl acceptable to the British society of the times.

When all hopes crashed and Christopher was left with no options, he met Lynette to tell her the decision. When he arrived, she was already waiting at their favourite table in the same restaurant where they had spent countless evenings. The dusky beauty in a pale lemon dress with red rose petals embroidered round the neck and black shining hair cascading down to her waist lifted her eyes and looked hopefully at him. But one glance at Christopher and she knew the decision. Both sat for hours without uttering a word. They ordered nothing, though Bashir Bearer remembered to bring for them their favourite chicken patties and cold coffee with ice cream which remained untouched till they left. Christopher had remembered, as always, to bring a string of bela flowers and put them in her hair. So long as belas were in bloom, a string of those fragrance emitting flowers had always been a daily present for Lynette's hair by Christopher. As they moved out of the restaurant they stopped briefly in the foyer and Christopher mumbled, 'I never knew we'd part like this. I thought it would be "till death do us part."'

And Lynette replied looking straight into his eyes, 'Don't worry Chris, now we'll be together beyond death, even death will not part us.' Christopher didn't understand and made no attempt to understand. Both walked out of the foyer and on to the road. As always Christopher took his cycle from the parking and started walking with Lynette towards her house which was a stone's throw from where they stood. 'I'll go alone, I just have a road to cross, you get along,' Lynette said and Christopher did not insist on accompanying her. He turned towards his house and cycled back home as though in a trance. And in a trance he remained for many months thereafter.

***

Marian had to drop her plans of settling in Scotland with her sons, due to the incidents that followed, but she insisted that Christopher complete his internship. With the help of some of his teachers she could convince him. It was in the hospital attached to the Medical College that he started his internship.

Not even two weeks had gone by when the Senior Superintendent, Dr Bannerji, while on an informal round, which he took late at night, heard strange sounds coming from Room Number 12 of the Special Ward. He knew it was unoccupied. All unoccupied rooms were kept locked. Dr. Bannerji noticed that that there was no lock on the door.

He turned the knob and found, to his great surprise, the door bolted from inside. Peeping from an unpainted window pane, he was horrified to see a person hanging from the fan. He raised an alarm. Two nurses and a ward boy came running. Together they broke open the door and entered the room.

They found Christopher lying on the bed. He was breathing and his eyes were open. Dr Bannerji, who was the first to enter, followed by the two nurses and the ward boy, was startled to see Christopher on the bed. He was absolutely sure he had seen someone hanging from the fan. Though he wasted no time to ensure that necessary medicines were administered to Christopher, his mind was in a turmoil. He just could not understand who could have untied the noose from his neck and laid him down on the bed. Dr Bannerji expressed his surprise. The two staff nurses and the ward boy had also not seen anyone else in the room. But the Matron who had followed them into the room said she did see Christopher's fiancée standing near the head of the bed. 'I watched her leave the room; as she turned to go I saw a string of bela flowers decorating her beautiful black hair.' Dr Bannerji listened with great care and then walked up to the Matron. 'Though I saw no one I also had felt that there was a fragrance of bela flowers in the room. I suggest you send for Dr Christopher Barret's mother and brother immediately. I am sure Christopher will survive, but it is a police case nevertheless, the presence of another person inside the room makes the case more complicated. I am surprised why I didn't notice the girl.'

'Doctor, you were in too much of a tension when you entered the room,' the Matron explained.

By the time his mother arrived, Christopher's condition was stable. But Dr Bannerji did not allow any questions to be put to him. Marian begged Dr Bannerji not to inform the police.

'Look Mrs Barret, if it was a simple case of an attempted suicide, I could have covered it up because Christopher is otherwise a very disciplined and able person. But it is a complicated matter. There was another person in the room. It is in Christopher's interest that we should get to the bottom of the case.'

'May I ask you Doctor, who was the other person in the room?' Christopher's mother asked.

'Well I didn't see, but Matron saw his fiancée standing at the head of his bed. And from the description she gave me, I too am sure she was his fiancée, I have seen her with him very often.'

'Impossible!' was Marian's one word retort.

'What do you mean Mrs Barret?' Dr Bannerji was not very pleased with her response.

'I can guarantee it was not his fiancée. Lynette was not there.' Marian Barret was in a state of shock.

'Compose yourself Mrs Barret, What makes you so sure that his fiancée was not in the room?' the doctor asked.

'Because his fiancée is dead, she died more than six months ago. And since then Christopher is breathing no doubt, but has no will to live.' And Mrs Marian Barret went on to tell the doctor and the matron the entire story. 'When they met for the last time in their favourite restaurant,' Marian Barret said, 'Lynette was wearing a pale yellow dress with rose petals embroidered on it and Christopher had, as usual, put a string of bela flowers on her black hair. She didn't allow him to reach her to her house. She said she had just a road to cross. But she couldn't cross that road. A station wagon hit her. She died on the spot. It was no suicide. She was obviously overwrought, not in her senses to notice the oncoming vehicle.'

The story left everyone in a state of shock. There was total silence for some time.

Dr Bannerji, the professional that he was, still wanted to know who brought him down from the fan to the bed. He asked Marian to find that out from her son.

'Christopher, darling, you were hanging from the fan weren't you?'

'Yes.'

'Who brought you down to the bed?'

'She ...' Christopher said and after a long pause continued, 'I now know what she meant when she said "Even death cannot part us."' There was a painful silence again.

A few weeks later Christopher recovered and to everyone's surprise regained his earlier cheerfulness. Dr Bannerji did not take the matter to the police, nor did he find any reason to take a promise from Christopher to respect the gift of life which God had bestowed upon him. Christopher's words and actions had, for some reason, started reflecting a greater zest for life than ever before.

He completed his internship and started his practice. For years thereafter he was seen cycling from basti to basti and village to village with his bag of medicines on the cycle carrier, bringing succour and hope to the poor. His brother Bryan, in the meanwhile, married and brought up a happy family. Though his mother Marian never came out of the shadow of fear after his suicide attempt, Christopher really lived life to the fullest. And he outlived them all.

Five decades later when he died, unwed and without a permanent home, at the ripe old age of seventy-seven he was followed to the cemetery by hordes of mourners from all walks of life. It was a cold December afternoon when he was laid to rest. In the midst of a scramble to throw a fistful of dust over his mortal remains, people suddenly saw a string of fresh bela flowers drop from someone's hand on to the coffin. A whiff of the heady fragrance of bela flowers enveloped the entire cemetery, filling mourners with wonder as to how nature could make bela flowers blossom on a severely cold December afternoon.

Centipede

Once the date for Asiya's wedding was fixed, arrangements for the ceremonies preceding the wedding began in all earnest. The womenfolk of the family got together to decide how long the period of the *manjha* should be. Asiya hoped it would be a short one. The date of the wedding was 8th July, if the period of the *manjha* was a long one, God forbid, the sweltering heat of June would be unbearable for her. It was not easy to sit all covered up in a curtained room with doors and windows closed for days and days, sometimes for more than a month. 'Baji, it is so hot, please see that the *manjha* is a short one,' Asiya whispered in her elder sister Abida's ear. Abida was married for four years. 'Don't worry,' Abida said, 'we have a table fan at home in Kanpur. When your Dulha Bhai comes he will bring it. Before I left for Lucknow I told him to do so.'

'What is the discussion about?' Asiya's mother's queried as she entered the room. With her was her sister who was married to her husband's younger brother. She carried a tray bearing a sweet smelling paste called *uptan*, to be applied on the bride's face and body everyday till the day of the wedding. 'What were you saying about a table fan, Abida?' Asiya's mother wanted to know what her daughters were talking about. 'Amma, actually it is very hot, nowadays. Keep that in mind when you decide the period of the *manjha*.'

'I am sure Asiya asked you to put in a word.' Her mother said with a frown on her face.

'Amma, don't I know how hot it is? Asiya doesn't have to tell me that,' Abida protested.

'The wedding is just round the corner and we all know that Asiya has still not stopped talking. After all she is the bride. It is most unbecoming for a bride to interfere or even utter a word about anything concerning her own wedding plans,' the mother said and added, 'Don't forget, an Indian bride's biggest ornament is her *sharam*, her *haya*, her shyness and timidity.'

'We are no enemies; we will keep the bride's comfort in mind,' that was the bride's aunt who accompanied Asiya's mother. Just then the grandmother of the bride also entered the room and announced that it was time for the *manjha* ceremony to begin. A lot of guests had come and were waiting in the veranda below.

'But we have yet not decided how long the bride will sit for the *manjha*,' Asiya's mother said.

'What is there to decide? Let her sit for as long as you sat. How long was your *manjha*?' The grandmother asked her daughter-in-law.

'Amma, it is very hot. This room where Asiya is sitting is hotter still. It has just one window and one door,' Asiya's mother said.

'One window and one door? How many windows and doors do you want the room to have? Does a bride sit in a *baradari*, a twelve-door pavilion, during her *manjha*?' the grandmother chided. 'My child, *manjha* is the time when the bride is kept in total seclusion. She is in purdah even from her own father and brothers and also from most women. When even close female family members come into the room to see her, she keeps her face covered and eyes closed. It is during this period that a young girl shows how a bride should behave. She should remain an embodiment of timidity throughout the period.'

'In fact, girls should not forget that they are girls all their lives. They should remain embodiments of shyness as long as they live. They will be respected only then,' The grandmother's sister, Kulsuman, added.

'You are right Amma; I only want the *manjha* period to be short. My *manjha* was for twenty one days. But that was a cooler month. We can't make Asiya sit in this room for that long in the sweltering heat of June.' Asiya's mother said.

'Dulhan is right, this summer is scorching. We can't have a long *manjha*,' the grandmother finally decided.

'Then should it be for fifteen days?' Kulsuman asked.

'That would also be too long in this weather, Kulsuman Khala.' Asiya's mother said.

'Alright. These are modern times, so we will reduce it to seven days.' The grandmother gave the final verdict.

The bride's sister and mother agreed readily.

But Kulsuman intervened addressing her sister, the bride's grandmother. 'But Apa do you realise that the *manjha* period is always till the wedding day? And there are still sixteen days left for the great day. Apa I think the *manjha* will have to be for fifteen days. On the sixteenth day, late in the evening, we will apply henna on Asiya's palms and feet.'

'Ya Allah, how could I have forgotten that? Old age makes one demented. Never mind, we'll stick to the seven day *manjha* and we'll start the ceremony next week.' The grandmother was firm.

'Apa, what's the matter with you? Really, old age has overpowered you. There are all told ten women and five girls you invited from the mohalla and from among our relatives. You have arranged for a glass of sherbet to be served to each of them. You'll ask them to go away and come back next week?' Kulsuman khala wanted to know.

'Yes I did invite them. And they'll leave only after having the sherbet and snacks and paan. It's only the *manjha* which will start next week. Look Kulsuman, I have promised the girl's mother that the *manjha* period will be short.' The grandmother added after a pause. 'And isn't this summer really severe? Why put the girl to extra trouble?'

'Apa you've really changed. What exactly do you mean by saying "why put the girl to extra trouble?" What extra trouble? We all have gone through that "trouble" during our time.' Kulsuman was determined to have a longer *manjha* period for Asiya. But the bride's grandmother had the last word. Asiya's mother and sister quickly got up and went into the courtyard and started serving sherbet and snacks to the guests who were waiting there. They also spread the word around that Asiya had developed a fever so the *manjha* would start next week. Some women looked disappointed, but others appeared more interested in the sherbet which came as a relief on that hot summer day.

'Apa you'll call these women again next week and add to the expenditure with another round of sherbet.' Kulsuman's persistence was incredible.

'Why should I?' Her sister replied.

'You will need seven suhagans, happily married women with husbands living, to apply *uptan* on Asiya.' Kulsuman informed.

'Yes of course! But I don't have to invite *suhagans* from other homes. Please God, we have seven *suhagans* right here, in this very house,' and she pointed out seven married women—herself and her sister Kulsuman, her two daughters, her two daughters-in-law and Abida, her granddaughter. All happily married women who had husbands alive and living with them. 'All these fortunate women will apply *uptan* with their auspicious hands on my dear Asiya. And one week with *uptan* massage will be enough to make her as beautiful as the moon,' she said and left the room to say Khuda Hafiz to the guests as they departed.

A week later the *manjha* ceremony started with the seven *suhagans*, all from the family, rubbing the *uptan* paste made of ground lentils mixed with almond oil on the bride dressed in a yellow coloured outfit as decreed by custom. After the *suhagans*, some young unmarried girls, friends of the bride, also applied the *uptan* on her hands and feet. The ceremony was not without music. Professional women singers called *mirasins* entertained the ladies with wedding songs and skits. Finally the barber's wife whom everyone addressed as *navan* gave her a thorough massage with the *uptan* paste. *Navan* repeated this procedure daily till the wedding. Few women and no man saw Asiya's face till after the wedding. While she sat, all covered and shrivelled up in one corner of the room women of the family would come and sit in the room and talk among themselves.

No one would address the bride and she never uttered a word of course. Though her eyes were closed her ears were not, so she could hear what her women relatives were talking about. One story which she repeatedly heard from almost all the women including her mother and her grandmother was the story of the bride and the centipede. Everyone knew, as also Asiya, that the story was narrated for her ears.

And the story was about a bride who had just entered her husband's home after their marriage and was sitting all dressed up in her red wedding dress while women were coming to see her face. Her husband's sister sat near her to lift her veil and show her face and also to collect the *munh dikhai* (literally money or gift for showing the face of the bride,) which the women guests gave. The *munh dikhai* ceremony lasted some time. The bride of course made no sound, kept her eyes lowered, but suddenly dropped dead into the lap of her sister-in-law. Actually a centipede had crawled inside her kurta and dug its multiple legs into her skin then into her flesh and then further and further into her body. The bride, the good girl that she was, knew the discipline a bride should follow. She knew that a bride couldn't be so shameless as to start screaming in front of everyone and announcing that there was something wriggling inside her kurta. She kept quiet and allowed the poisonous tentacles of the centipede to do the mischief. She preferred death over shamelessness!

Asiya had heard this story many times before, but this time it gave her nightmares. She dreaded the thought of a centipede coming anywhere near her, leave alone getting inside her clothes. She was sure she would let off a scream before fainting even if she was in the midst of a gathering of her in-laws. It was the scream and the subsequent bad reputation which she dreaded, not so much the fainting or collapsing as a consequence. But thank God, the *manjha*, the wedding and the first visit to her husband's home, all went off well. Thankfully no centipede appeared and her reputation as a shy bride remained intact.

The year of Asiya's wedding was 1949. Her husband was only a student then. When he completed his studies they crossed over to Pakistan and settled down in Karachi. That was where she brought up her family. But when her sons grew up and completed their education they bid goodbye to Pakistan and found their way to Canada. She visited them several times but refused to make Canada her home. 'Spare me the torture of settling in the West. The culture of the place makes the girls too shameless.' That was the reason which Asiya gave for not settling with her sons in Canada. Her sons always remembered their mother saying that if she ever got a chance to go back to Lucknow and settle there, she would grab the opportunity. Her husband shared her views. Actually Asiya had visited her parents and other family members in Lucknow only once after crossing over to Pakistan. And when the children came, it became all the more difficult for her to take any trips out of Karachi. With her husband's limited salary it was just possible to somehow scrape through and just ensure the children's education. Their budget could support nothing more. Tours and holidays were out of question. But now things were different. All their responsibilities were over. Their sons were doing well and were very supportive. Her husband's pension and all his post-retirement benefits had made them quite prosperous.

Asiya's two younger brothers had followed them to Pakistan after graduating from Lucknow University and had settled down in Karachi. But Asiya hadn't met Abida, her elder sister, for more than fifty years. Abida lived in Lucknow after her husband's death. Both the sisters were getting along in age and wanted to see each other desperately.

***

Providence decided in their favour and the two sisters were together once again more than fifty years later, in their very own

Lucknow. They laughed and giggled like teenagers despite their advancing years, remembering the events of their youth. They went to see their old house in Mamu Bhanje ki Qabar. They were not so disappointed to see the old house, which though dilapidated, could be recognised. But when they passed Kallan ki Lat, they were horrified to see the European cemetery which they remembered as a large beautiful park with obelisk shaped graves scattered between tall shady trees. The obelisks had been pulled down and an ugly jumble of shanties stood in their place.

'The old part of Lucknow was a disappointment Baji, though that is the real Lucknow. It is surprising why nothing could be done to maintain it. Even the Imambaras lie neglected,' Asiya said when they came back home.

'What do you say about the new part of Lucknow?' her nephew asked.

'That is new dear, not the Lucknow I knew, not my Lucknow,' Asiya said.

'Come on Khala jaan, from the airport to Gomtinagar, Lucknow can be easily compared to Paris.' Abida's son wanted to rekindle Asiya's interest in Lucknow.

'Maybe, but my Lucknow looks old and haggard,' Asiya said, 'or am I looking at it with my cataract ridden eyes?'

'Exactly. For once you are right,' Asiya's husband said. 'I was smarter, just before leaving for Lucknow I got my cataract operation done, in both the eyes. No part of Lucknow looks old and haggard to me. It looks as young and sprightly as it did on the day when I led my *baraat* to your house!' Everyone laughed and the mood of the evening became pleasant again.

'So Khala jaan, would you still prefer to settle down in Lucknow if the Indian Government allows you?' Asiya's nephew asked.

'Yes,' Asiya said without any hesitation.

A week later her nephew offered to take her and his mother to the wedding of a friend's daughter. 'We are invited to all the ceremonies, Khala jaan.'

'No Beta, I won't go. Your family doesn't mean guests also.'

'Khala jaan, we are very close, our families know each other from the time of Nana Abba, your father. Ammi told me that you people kind of knew each other,' the nephew said.

'Remember Asiya there was a Maulana Ahmad Husain who used to visit Abba very often in his *baithak* downstairs. The bride is his granddaughter, the bride's father Shujauddin is a PCS officer,' Abida tried to remind her sister.

'I think I remember. Abba used to say that the Maulana is very highly educated but too orthodox,' Asiya said.

'Oh yes, you are right. Asiya, you have an excellent memory.' Abida was really surprised at Asiya's instant recall.

Asiya at last consented to go to the wedding and other ceremonies. First was the *manjha* which was at the Taj Hotel. The whole family landed up at the five-star Hotel. The older people, particularly Asiya and Abida, were very impressed with the parents of the bride.

'They have booked rooms here for the *manjha* so that their daughter may not go through the rigours of the weather,' Asiya said and both sisters remembered that boiling month of June when Asiya spent seven days bundled up in that small room which was really no room but a kind of storage space with hardly any ventilation. 'Times have changed, there are more facilities now and don't forget, these parents are far richer than our parents could ever have been,' Abida said.

'Don't be in such a hurry, Ammi, to find excuses for your parents' inability to book air-conditioned rooms for your *manjha*. There were no five-star hotels in the pre independence period in Lucknow when you got married and air-conditioning was unheard of. Even these parents have not booked any rooms for their daughter's comfort. This hall alone has been hired for the evening, for the comfort of the invitees,' Abida's son informed.

Abida and Asiya sat with the rest of the family and waited for the *manjha* ceremony to start. The chairs were laid as though in an auditorium. Before them was a large platform built like a stage. On one side was the band.

Soon there was an announcement that the programme is about to start with a solo dance performance by the bride's sister. The anchor said a lot of nice things about her before she appeared on stage and danced to a film song. After her, two groups of girls performed. The first group were the sister's friends. The second performance was that of the bride's friends. And lo and behold, next appeared the bride herself! She came on the stage, to the wild clapping of her friends, dressed in a shimmering lehnga and a matching blouse which revealed more than it covered. She wriggled like mad and moved each part of her body to the music, to such an extent, that not only Asiya and Abida, but the rest of the audience too, sat stuck to their chairs dumbfounded.

When Asiya recovered from the shock, she asked just three questions, one shorter than the other –

'Is she really the bride?'

'Is this her *manjha*?'

'Is this Lucknow?'

And then she found the answer herself –

'I bet, she was wriggling on the stage, because the centipede had crawled into her blouse through its many windows!'

A Word Thrice Uttered

Even bad luck does not come without being invited, whether you invite her willingly or under compulsion. Kausar was forced to send an invitation to bad luck when she married a man socially, financially and educationally much below the status and standing of her own family. There was no roof over her head, nor over that of her disabled child and yet no member of her own kin was willing to give her shelter or support.

As luck would have it, Kausar soon started feeling that she was perhaps better off at her brother's house despite the taunts and jibes of her brother and sister-in-law and the insulting glances of her nieces. Or she could have taken up his offer of setting up a separate establishment for her, despite the inconvenience.

In this marriage she had lost all her dignity and respect, something she still had at her brother's place despite the insults and innuendos. Her husband and his sister would beat her up and also her innocent little child at the least excuse. To top it, each time her husband screamed at her or beat her he'd always issue an ultimatum, 'If you do not mend your ways soon,

I'll utter that word thrice! And off you'll find yourself on the streets! With nothing in your hands but a bowl.' And from the other side his sister would add coolly and cruelly, 'You know Kausar, you've no one in this whole world who will take you in, even for a day. Why don't you mend your ways and learn to serve your husband the way he deserves? Supposing he utters that word thrice! What will you do? Where will you go?'

A year later the husband put the child in an orphanage for disabled children. Kausar was sad at the separation but thought that it was better than having the child in that torture cell where destiny had dumped her. She was allowed to visit her child only if the brute she married was willing. Years went by with her luck never taking a turn for the better.

Kausar even forgot the happy days she enjoyed in Lucknow and Nainital, her school friends, her stepmother's highly educated uncles and cousins. Though she could never open up fully with her stepmother and father, yet she realised what an elegant and charming couple they were. People only spoke in soft tones in her home. There was no fighting ever in those serene surroundings, no raised voices, no harsh words.

'And now I'm 65 years old, ma'am. My bones are too weak to bear the beatings I'm daily exposed to. Even as a child my parents never beat me nor allowed anyone else to even touch me. My stepmother didn't address a single harsh word to me,' Kausar was sharing her woes with a lady retired from government service who lived in a flat so close that she was witness to the goings on in Kausar's life.

Whenever the lady found Kausar alone, which was very seldom, she spoke kind words of comfort and concern to her. She also advised her to walk out on the man putting aside her fear that she had no one in the world. She kept reassuring her that someone or the other would come to her aid, would stand up for her. Her nephews and nieces were still there. One of them would show compassion, hold her hand and pull her out of the bog and morass that she had sunk into.

'Next time he threatens to utter that word defy him to do so, to utter it thrice, and then just walk out, if he does so,' the lady suggested.

'Supposing he takes that as impertinence on my part, beats me up even more soundly, or, God forbid, kills me, what will happen to my poor son?'

'Dear Kausar, for once, set your fears aside and put your trust in God. He will help you,' The old lady's words gave Kausar unusual strength. She could feel determination seeping into her being and enveloping it.

Opportunity was, as if, waiting for her in the wings. Her husband gave her a button to stitch on to his shirt. When she gave it to him after putting the button on, he took off his shoe and started hitting her with it. 'You'll never learn anything. I'll not give you any more leeway. The time has come for me to utter that word.'

Before he knew what was happening, she snatched the shoe from his hand, threw it at him and shouted, 'Don't keep threatening, *lillah* utter it. And utter it *thrice*.'

'Do you know what you are saying,' said the man, surprised, completely taken aback.

'I'm dying to hear those words. Their utterance is the key to my release from this hell,' Kausar said emphatically.

'Teach the slut a lesson, say it loud and clear.' His sister screamed, egging him on from the other end of the room.

The husband was now not going to keep his right unused. 'Talaq, Talaq, Talaq,' he roared. It was 10:45 pm.

Those three words were the cue for Kausar to get up and leave. She went down the steps, calmly and determinedly, without looking back even once. The husband watched, mute and wide-eyed, shock paralysing him. As Kausar descended the steps, his expression turned to horror. Had he actually wasted the *three most powerful words*, his ammunition, his only hold over her till now?

By 10:47 pm she was on the road. The good old lady of her neighbourhood was waiting for her. She had decided she would be the saviour and give Kausar immediate help, so that her promise of God helping Kausar, if she was brave-hearted to walk out, held true.

***

Kausar's mother Zarina was her father Rashid's second wife, a girl he never wanted to marry when his first wife died. But everyone in his family and that of his wife's were bent upon thrusting her on him because she was the first wife's sister and all relatives were sure that she would look after his motherless children with care and love for they were her sister's children too. For many years he avoided the marriage but couldn't finally go against his parents' wishes. Those were the times when young men and women had no say in deciding who their life partners should or would be. Rashid worked as a senior clerk in a government office in Lucknow, while his parents and children lived in their ancestral home in Bareilly.

It is not Rashid's story or Zarina's that I am going to tell but the story of Kausar. A story which neither began on a truly happy note nor had any happy landmarks. India, or should I say the subcontinent, abounds with such stories of women who had either no one to empower them or those who let opportunities slip like sand through their fingers.

Before I embark on Kausar's story, there is a fragment still left to be told of her father's narrative which is a vital part of her story too. The reason for her father avoiding his second marriage with his sister-in-law was his fondness for a very young girl called Amina who lived, with her family, in his neighbourhood in Lucknow. The young girl too had a soft spot for him. A few months after his first wife died he had spoken to the girl's parents about his intentions to marry her. They had shown their willingness, but had insisted that his parents should come down to Lucknow with the proposal.

Obviously the parents never came. Rashid was hardly a widower for a little more than two years when his parents' were successful in prevailing upon him to marry the girl of their choice. The next year he was a father once again to another daughter – Kausar.

This important development in his life, he disclosed to no one in Lucknow, not even to the family where a young girl was waiting patiently, for his parents to arrive with a proposal.

Mir Sahib, the girl's father, was getting restless. At last he questioned Rashid and told him that he could not wait any longer since he had two more daughters to settle apart from the one Rashid wanted to marry. It was then that Rashid owned up and revealed the latest developments in his life. The old man was livid. To crown it all Rashid said that he was still eager to marry Amina and promised to keep her happy. Mir Sahib got up in a huff, came back home and shared the disgraceful news with his wife.

But they were put to greater shame when their daughter turned around and said that she would marry no one else but

Rashid. Thankfully she laid down a condition for Rashid too. He had to set her up in an independent establishment of her own in Lucknow. And she would never have anything to do with his other wife or his family. Rashid agreed to her conditions and they got married. Surprisingly, Amina, as Rashid's third wife, was very happy. Over time, Mir Sahib and the rest of the family also became very fond of him and had cordial relations with him.

Zarina, the older wife, continued to live with his parents and little Kausar in Bareilly. All this happened around the dawn of independence, when even government servants could marry more than once, regardless of the faith they subscribed to.

All was hunky dory till Zarina was alive! Unfortunately she died when Kausar was just eight. By then Rashid's parents had also passed away. His daughter by his first wife had got married to a senior bureaucrat in Delhi and his son was settled in Mumbai. Rashid had no other option but to bring Kausar to live with him and Amina, in Lucknow. Amina saw, in the eight year old child, the face of her mother, Rashid's other wife. And that was reason enough for her to dislike Kausar.

They couldn't have been a happy set of constellations under which Kausar was born, poor child. Within days of her birth her father had wed another wife. Even while her mother was alive she lived a deprived childhood. She longed to see both her parents together. She wished she could play in her father's lap like other children did, but had to be content with mere glimpses of him during his flying visits. Even before she could understand what death was, she was brought face to face with her mother's death. And her dream to see her parents together remained unrealised, like so many other dreams she wove for herself as life moved on.

Truth be told, Rashid was no monster. He ensured that his daughter got everything she needed – good clothes, good food, toys, holidays. He saw that her stepmother didn't ill treat her. But he could not somehow befriend her. And Kausar too remained hesitant to speak out her mind either to him or to her stepmother from whom she hardly ever got an approving glance. But she made friends easily with Amina's relatives and giggled and joked when she was alone with them, which was not very often, thanks to the rules laid down by her stepmother.

Kausar's biggest drawback was that she was not very good at her studies. With great difficulty she scraped through Intermediate examination. Beyond that she could not proceed. But she had an interest in household chores. When she first came to Lucknow she was fascinated by the lovely chikan embroidery her stepmother used to do and was quite impressed with her tailoring and cooking too. She wished she could also try her hand at all that work. 'Ammi teach me how to make all those flowers with needle and thread,' the little child once asked her stepmother in an endearingly pleading tone.

'I don't have any time to waste on children like you; you can learn it all in school. It was there that I learnt all that. My mother didn't teach me,' Amina said, a frown creasing her brow with wrinkles. Kausar thought she had trespassed into a field she was not supposed to enter. Similarly in the arena of the kitchen, Amina once said, without realising that her husband was within earshot, 'Kausar go and study. Your father does not want you to waste your time in the kitchen,' when Kausar was trying her hand at chapatti-making.

'I never meant that she should never even try to learn. Yes we should not impose the burden of the kitchen on her,' Rashid clarified, irritation tingeing his voice.

'Today we have guests for dinner. She can try her hand at cooking some other day.' Amina never got into an argument with her husband.

So, to start with, Kausar was given cooking and housekeeping lessons by her stepmother, more in deference to her husband's wishes than any real affection or concern. Her interest in teaching was roused, however, when she found Kausar a fast learner. She then taught her stitching and embroidery too. Kausar was by now a young lady of marriageable age. She was not beautiful but not bad-looking either; not tall and trim, but short and petite.

Her father had long retired, though as a gazetted officer, but did not have many connections in the society that mattered. It was not within his reach to get a husband of the same status for Kausar as he was able to find for his older daughter. But he was hopeful that his daughter and son-in-law would step in and help. His son too was working with an airline, in a position high enough to be able to find a match for Kausar.

Rashid was right. His son-in-law was able to find a suitable boy for Kausar. The young man, named Masoud, was a journalist who worked in an Urdu newspaper. Though the Urdu newspaper was not paying him well, Rashid approved of the match because the boy's parents were well off and Kausar had herself been educated at an Urdu school. Everyone thought they would make a well matched couple and rightly so.

Rashid spent all his savings on the wedding much against the wishes of his wife Amina. 'Don't worry Amina, my pension is enough for both of us; and I wonder if you know, after I am no more, the government will give you a family pension all your life,' Rashid tried to pacify her.

'You misunderstand me. I am not worried about myself or my needs. My worry is that the boy, going by the elaborate celebrations and the status of our elder son-in-law, may think we are very rich and start nursing expectations from us even later,' Amina said.

The wedding went off well. The boy's family appeared quite happy because they had acquired good connections through marriage with Kausar. Not very long after, Masoud got a permanent government job, in the Urdu section of All India Radio, thanks to the intervention of Rashid's older son-in-law. Within a year and a half of marriage, a son was born to the couple. Rashid felt that Kausar had finally got all that she needed and deserved, for a full and fruitful life. He was indeed a happy man when he died, four years later. Humans have no sight which can peer into the future. It is the present which determines their joy or sorrow. Maybe rightly and thankfully so. The events that unfolded later would have torn his heart apart.

It was sometime after Rashid died that Kausar's son fell seriously ill. His temperature shot up and did not come down, even with medications, for some time. Finally, with expert medical help the child survived, but a part of his brain, which controlled the speech centre, was permanently damaged. The boy was physically fit but he became mentally retarded and had no speech. Kausar was shattered.

Sometime later her husband came home one day from office and said, 'You know Kausar, the B.B.C. has advertised for the post of Producer for their Urdu Programmes. I fulfil all the criteria. If I get someone to pursue my case there, I'll get the job.'

Kausar was dejected. 'Why go away so far, let's stick to our own country. Baji and Bhaisahib are here; your relatives are also near us.'

'You know Kausar I'm told medical facilities in Britain are far advanced. Our son can get treatment from the best brain surgeons there. With luck they can even reverse the damage to his brain. If I can get a job there, our child's life will bloom forth once again,' Masoud said with such sincerity that Kausar immediately stood up and said, 'Let's go to Baji. Let's see if something can be done.'

Her sister, whom she called Baji, had the key to all problems because of her well-placed husband. This time too she had a solution, though her husband, obviously, couldn't do anything in another country. She remembered that their first cousin was in England and working with the B.B.C. Though their cousin wrote back as frankly as he could that job selections in that country were done on the basis of merit, he did not discourage Kausar's husband from sending in his bio-data. He also informed in the same letter that he himself was leaving England and settling down in the USA. But the cousin's presence at that time and his long stint in the Organisation did help, directly or indirectly. Masoud got the job.

Masoud wasted no time in getting his travel documents prepared and leaving the shores of India. Before he left he packed off Kausar and the child to Mumbai. 'You must go and spend some time with your brother and his family, I'll soon be sending your visa. Once you join me there, it will be a long time before you can see your relatives again,' he said.

Kausar was hardly there in Mumbai for twenty days when an envelope addressed to her came by post. It was her husband Masoud's letter from England. She was delighted. She could hardly wait to open it. But when she read it she found, it was not a letter but a declaration of Talaq, with reasons why it was not possible for Masoud to carry on conjugal relations with her. She almost collapsed. Her brother and sister-in-law took the letter to many Moulvis and Ulemas who said the divorce was valid. Her sister took the case to court, but to no avail. The parents of Masoud were apparently apologetic but refused to have anything to do with her or her child. They said that all her belongings had been taken away by Masoud and that they had nothing to give back.

Kausar's brother-in-law had in the meanwhile complained to the External Affairs Ministry that Masoud had cheated his wife and her family. As a result the BBC dismissed Masoud from service and he was forced to return to India. But the divorce was not declared invalid. Kausar was not given any damages. She was not given any maintenance for her son either. She felt she was trapped in a pitch dark tunnel with no light and no end in sight either.

She stayed on with her brother who maintained warmth in the beginning. But when his wife showed her resentment, his attitude too became cold and distant. Kausar started stitching clothes for people in the neighbourhood, so that she could contribute something to the budget. Her earnings were, naturally, meagre. One day her sister-in- law told her, 'No use working all day. The money you give me does not even cover the amount I pay for the milk your child has.' Kausar was aware that her earning from stitching and tailoring was a pittance. She was also aware that she was neither educated enough nor had any special skills or proficiency to earn more than what she did, though, had she been given time, she could have established herself in the tailoring business. But none in the family had any patience with her. Even her sister, who had come to Mumbai for consulting an Oncologist, gave reasons for her inability to help. She was in the last stages of cancer, all her attention was focussed on fighting the disease. She expressed her helplessness and told Kausar, very frankly, that her husband and sons were not willing to keep her and her son with them in Delhi and also told her categorically that all they could do, they had already done for her.

After some time her sister-in-law took away her sewing machine and said if she wanted to stitch something she should go to her ex-husband's house and get back her things from them, knowing full well that all that had been unsuccessfully tried before. Her brother even blamed their father for having given her much more at her wedding than he spent on his education, and that he had never given anything to his wife. Poor Kausar found herself a job in a factory which made purses, where she earned just a few rupees more, though she was very good with her hands and was quite an asset to the factory.

Despite her requests, the owner never obliged her with a raise in her wages. After a few months, he, however, proposed to her! Kausar refused. She couldn't think of another marriage after the first disastrous one. But she couldn't find another job and had to continue in the same factory. The owner proposed yet again! This time he raised her wages also, but very nominally. Kausar refused. But things in her brother's home were getting more difficult. Her retarded son was becoming an embarrassment to his children and the child's constant illness was a drain on her brother's purse which his wife resented.

Finally her brother suggested that it was time she shifted to some other place. He promised to provide her some financial support. But that support was too insufficient even to rent a room in a chawl. There was no one else who was willing to accommodate her. Her stepmother was dead by then. Maybe she could have found a home with her stepmother, but as fate would have it, that was not to be. It was at that juncture, driven by utter despair, that she thought of accepting the factory owner's proposal.

She put the matter before her brother who was indifferent and apathetic, totally unconcerned. He merely said, 'Do what you please,' washing his hands off the matter. Her sister and brother-in-law were also noncommittal. There was an uncle still alive. He advised her to keep away from marriage but could offer no viable alternative for her livelihood. So Kausar was driven by destiny to fall into the abyss of bad luck that had laid a trap for her. She walked straight into the trap, eyes fully open, hoping for the best, hoping against hope for a turn of luck.

***

Kausar was relieved to see the neighbour, for though she had walked out boldly after her husband had uttered 'Talaq' thrice, she was quaking inside wondering what more, by way of further ill luck, destiny had in store for her.

'Good you took my advice and rid yourself of that fiend. I have thought of a place for you for the night. I will take you to my sister's flat. Tomorrow we'll decide about your future. Don't worry, as I said, God will have some plans for you,' the neighbour said reassuringly. Both started walking on.

They had hardly walked for half a kilometre when a car stopped near them asking for directions to some place. When Kausar turned around, she saw the lady's face and recognised her. She was the Director of the home where her son was admitted.

'Oh Kausarji! you haven't come for quite some time to see your son. You know, I was looking for you,' she said.

'Why, is my son unwell or something?'

'No, no, he is fine. Actually I was looking for you as I had a job in mind for you,' the lady replied.

Kausar was too stunned to respond but her neighbour had the presence of mind to enquire about the job.

'Well, she will have to look after special children, like her son. She'll get food, a place to stay, a regular monthly salary and above all, a bonus.'

'What is the bonus?' It was Kausar who asked this time around.

'To be always with your son,' the Director said and smiled. Both Kausar and the neighbour clapped their hands with joy.

'When can you join?'

'Right now. May I?' said Kausar and when the Director nodded, stepped into the car. She pulled her neighbour also inside the car, requesting the Director, 'Ma'am can my friend also be with me tonight?'

'Sure, no problem. Are you scared?'

'Not for myself. For her. I think her life is in danger tonight. I'll tell you about it later.'

***

Sometimes the worst of misfortunes, the deadliest blows of fate, can be the precursors to the advent of good luck and the light at the end of the tunnel. Kausar was sixty-five when she saw that glorious light. And she and her son lived happily ever after.

Sona and Tiger

Mohalla Sufiyan in Ludhiana was on the Grand Trunk Road, very close to the Arya School. Most of the families who lived here were related or known for generations to each other. Akbari and her husband Abid Husain lived in this mohalla with their three daughters, a son and a cow called Sona, who was like a fifth child for Akbari. Soon a dog called Tiger also came to live with the family. Abid Husain worked as a senior clerk in the Postal department. In the 1930s there were not many girls who went to school from that mohalla. But Akbari and Abid Husain took great pride in sending their three daughters to school. Their son Bashir was the youngest among their children. He went to the nearby Arya School.

Akbari had a very happy relationship with her daughters. She would often tease them. 'You know, dear girls, I'll never miss you when you are married and settled in your husbands' homes. Sona will be there to keep me company as she does now, when all of you are in school and your Abbaji is in his office,' she would say. And the girls would also tease her in return.

'In that case Bebe you better start calling Sona into the kitchen from now on to cook the meals,' Amtul the youngest would say for it was she who helped her mother to prepare breakfast and lunch before she left for school.

'And to wash clothes,' chirped Akhtar the eldest, who did all the washing and drying of clothes.

'Bebe you're sure to miss us, if not for anything else, at least for the work we do.' That was Maryam, the second daughter. Jokes apart, there was no one in the family who did not love Sona. But for Akbari, Sona was as dear as a daughter.

Sona came to Akbari's home as a present for Bashir. His friend Daljit's mother Rano gifted Sona to Bashir. Rano had come one day to their house to see Bashir, when he was down with typhoid.

'Behenji,' she addressed Akbari, 'Bashir is too thin. I don't think you give him enough milk.'

'No, Ranoji. That is not right. He starts his day with a big glass of milk and has one in the evening too,' Akbari said.

'Then it couldn't be pure milk. Where do you get the milk from?' Rano asked.

'From a milkman. He comes to my door to deliver it.' Akbari answered patiently.

'Behenji, you cannot trust these milkmen. Their milk is half water and half milk. They will not give pure milk even to their mother if she has to buy it from them,' Rano insisted.

'There is no other option; where else can you buy the milk from?'

'Why? Can't you keep a cow?' Rano asked.

'That is quite a hassle; you have to hire someone to milk it, to clean the place and pat cowdung cakes,' Akbari said.

'That's no problem. You can learn to milk a cow yourself. I will teach you. It'll take just a day to learn. And there is no dearth of sweepers looking for jobs. Anyone will clean up the place for a small payment. Offer them the cowdung too. They'll do the work more willingly.' Then she turned around to Bashir and said, 'Bashir you will get a present from me soon. I'll give you a beautiful calf, but you will have to help your mother to look after her. She will grow up very fast. And then you will have buckets of milk and butter and ghee in this very house. Your mother will make kheer and halwa and barfi every day for you to eat. But the condition is that you get well fast.' The good woman said so and left. Within two months time she came again and handed Sona to Bashir. With Sona came a lot of happiness for the family.

For a month or two, Sona remained inside the house. Then Akbari and her daughters built a cowshed for her near the big neem tree on the vacant space that was attached to their house. In the beginning Sona refused to shift to the cowshed. But when Akbari and her husband pulled their cots into the shed and spent a few nights there, she settled down happily.

Rano was right. Sona grew very fast. She just transformed from a cute little calf into a grown up cow in a blink. And soon she was a mother. A period of plenty followed for Akbari's household. Akbari would often say, 'My house has become Jannat with streams of milk flowing all over.' Ties of friendship between Rano's and Akbari's families too became stronger.

And one winter afternoon Bashir returned from school with a small white puppy. It couldn't have been more than a week old.

'Why did you bring him away from his mother? You naughty little boy,' Akbari chided Bashir.

'This puppy's mother is dead, Bebe, we must keep him with us.'

'No you can't, dogs shouldn't be kept in people's homes,' Akbari explained.

'Please Bebe let me keep him. Why can't I keep him?' Bashir insisted.

'Alright go and ask your father,' Akbari was too busy to argue with her son. In minutes Bashir brought his father, who was sitting in the sun reading a newspaper, to plead his case. 'Bebe, Abbaji says I can keep the puppy.'

'Let him keep the little creature, if the poor thing is left alone, he will die.' Akbari's husband knew his son's mind and he saw no point in wasting time trying to convince him.

Akbari was now saddled with the sixth child. And feeding this one was by no means an easy task. Initially she dipped wads of cotton wool in milk and squeezed the milk in the puppy's mouth. This helped to some extent. She would gently open his mouth and Bashir would squeeze the milk from the wad of cotton into it. Sometimes too much milk would go into the mouth and the puppy would start coughing. Feeding that way could cause choking; Akbari thought and consulted Rano, who suggested that the puppy be put near Sona's udders. That worked. The puppy started suckling Sona's milk. And the biggest miracle was, Sona did not mind, nor did her two month old calf.

The second day Sona started licking the puppy. After that, feeding him was no problem at all.

In a month's time he was a robust little puppy playing around Sona, taking more liberties with her than her own calf did. And he was given a majestic name too and that was Tiger. Like a tiger he became the king of the place. No one could enter the cowshed except the immediate family and woe betides anyone who dared touch Sona. The only person who was allowed to milk Sona was Akbari. Tiger refused to let even Taboo the sweeper clean the place. Somehow Bashir would cajole him to let Taboo in. But that was possible only if Bashir remained there, as long as Taboo did his work. Surprisingly even Sona would not let Tiger out of her sight. After he joined the family, Sona was never seen sitting alone.

Tiger created hell for the family once when Akbari developed a fever and a neighbour was requested to milk Sona. Bashir accompanied him into the cowshed. But he did not realise the intensity of Tiger's possessiveness for Sona. The neighbour had hardly put his hand on Sona when Tiger pounced on him and bit him. The poor fellow had to be given fourteen injections in his stomach after which he swore not to have anything to do with Akbari and her family. The matter did not end there. The entire Mohalla Sufiyan gathered outside Akbari's house and demanded that either Tiger be shot or sent far away to a place from where he would not be able to find his way back. Abid Husain had no other option but to give in to the demands of people of his mohalla. Tiger was really dangerous. Akbari's and his children's tears had to be ignored. He put Tiger in a sack and gave the sack to Taboo along with some money.

'Taboo, rent a cycle and go at least five miles from here. Let Tiger out of the sack only at a place from where you are sure he will not be able to come back.'

As Taboo left with the sack, Akbari and her family, including Abid Husain, wailed as anyone would when the dead body of a dear child leaves home on its last journey.

The family chulha lay unlit that evening. There was an awful silence in the house broken only by a sob from one of the children and a heart-piercing wail from Sona in the cowshed.

But the new day dawned with a smile for the family. After the Fajir Namaz, Akbari went out into the cowshed to be with Sona. Lo and behold! What does she see before her? Dear little Tiger and Sona licking each other's faces. Akbari gave out a shriek of ecstasy and the children as well as their father came rushing out of the house and into the cowshed. They stood transfixed to the ground, tears clouding their eyes. When Tiger saw the whole family standing there he came to them, wagging his tail. He stood on his hind legs and reached for Abid Husain's face and started licking it.

'Don't you know, dear Tiger, that it was this very sinner who sent you on an exile, away from your mother Sona and your home,' Abid Husain, was speaking to Tiger, tears streaming down his face. But Tiger was not listening. He didn't care. He was too happy to be back home with his mother and with those whom he loved. And so was everyone else. The whole Mohalla Sufiyan was taken by surprise but was not angry to see Tiger back. They never asked Abid Husain to send him away again.

But Sona and Tiger did not live happily ever after. For a long enough time, yes. But good times, like everything good, come to an end. After a few years Sona fell ill. There was just one veterinary hospital in Ludhiana in those days and that was a government hospital. Abid Husain got the senior-most vet from there to examine their dear Sona. But even he was not able to diagnose correctly. No one was able to make out that stones had developed in her bladder. Passing urine had become difficult for her. A lot of money was spent but Sona got no relief because the treatment was wrong. At last Sona died fighting pain. And it was pain she left behind for Akbari and her family.

And what did she leave behind for Tiger? Nothing. There was not a whimper from Tiger after Sona breathed her last.

Akbari's family wanted to bury Sona in the cowshed, but they were not allowed to do so. Though the land was attached to their house it did not belong to them. The body of Sona had to be handed over to the municipality employees who took it away on a hand pulled cart. Even when the cart was pulled away Tiger showed no resistance. He quietly followed the cart. Bashir wanted to stop him but Abid Husain told him not to. 'Kake let him go. Don't worry, he will come back.'

'Abbaji, it's so hot today.'

'It was hotter on the day when Taboo dropped him more than five miles away in the wilderness. Didn't he come back?'

But Tiger didn't come back. The following morning Abid Husain hired a tonga and left with Bashir and Rano's husband Surjit to the Dead Animal Yard which the Municipality had laid out at one end of the town.

There were not many dead animals there except a large black horse. Bashir spotted Sona. She lay not far from him. Round her neck was Tiger's forearm. His face rested on Sona's face. Both were fast asleep.

Gangaji Is Not Far, Bappa ...

Ram Khilawan was just ten when his father Gayadeen got a job for him at Unnao, with a school headmaster's family. The Headmaster's wife and elder widowed sister were also school teachers. All three worked in government schools and lived with their mother who looked after her son's children when the parents were away at school. After Ram Khilawan joined, all work concerning the children became his responsibility. He also swept the floor and helped in the kitchen. For his pains he was given ₹ 30 a month and two meals. In the morning, when the family had their breakfast of tea and chapattis, Ram Khilawan was also given his share. The family promised two sets of new clothes for him at Holi and Diwali. Gayadeen was satisfied. In his opinion, Ram Khilawan was fairly well looked after.

Gayadeen knew that Ram Khilawan was more responsible than most boys of his age, and yet he told him, as a parting advice, not to give his masters any trouble. Before dropping him at his master's house, he made Ram Khilawan promise that he would never touch anything unless he was asked to, never speak unless he was spoken to, never repeat anything which he heard at his master's house. Above all, he was told never to tell lies, and never to steal, not even food, even if he was starving. In return, his father promised that he would come and see him every day for the first week. And in that week if he found the work or family too difficult to cope with, he would take him back home.

For Ram Khilawan living away from home, with unfamiliar people, who were not his equals but his masters, was not easy. But even at that tender age he could guess that his father took the decision to send him to work under very difficult circumstances. He decided to pull on and told his father so. Gayadeen had got to know the headmaster because he and his nephew had done the whitewashing of the government school, where the headmaster was employed. By the time Ram Khilawan decided to stay on, Gayadeen's whitewashing work in Unnao was complete, so he stopped coming to see his son every day. But he came every month, riding ten kilometres on his cycle, to collect his son's wages. Ram Khilawan would jump with joy when his father came but when he turned to go back, the ten year old stood speechless looking longingly at him, hoping for the impossible to happen. Ram Khilawan learnt all too soon that the impossible never happens no matter how much one wants it to happen. He became aware that in the job which he held, going home was to be decided not by him or his father, but by the masters. The conditions of his job included three visits home in a year: one at Holi the second at Raksha Bandhan and the third at Diwali.

Ram Khilawan had no other option but to concentrate on his work which was supervised by the headmaster's mother. He made sure that she was never dissatisfied with him. She reminded him of his grandmother but he didn't dare take any liberties with her, though he called her Ammaji after taking her permission. That was what her children and grandchildren called her too. Ram Khilawan had hardly worked with the family for a month when Ammaji sent him to the halwai shop to get eight annas worth of jalebis. The halwai gave him nine jalebis which he brought home and placed in Ammaji's hands. Ammaji gave three each to her grandchildren. They grabbed the jalebis from her hands and gobbled them up immediately. She gave three to Ram Khilawan too. Ram Khilawan spread both his hands and took them but looked up at her for further instructions.

'These are for you, Ram Khilawan,' she told him.

'You haven't kept any for Bhaiyyaji, Bhabhiji and Didiji.'

'So what, they are adults,' she told him.

'I am also an adult,' he said.

'No, you are not. You're only a little older than them.' Ammaji said, pointing towards her grandchildren.

'Ammaji you haven't had any either. Please take from my share.' Ram Khilawan offered.

'Ram Khilawan, you eat all the three. Next time when I have saved more money I will give you one full rupee to buy jalebis and then the whole family will eat the sweets.'

Ram Khilawan put the jalebis in his mouth but it was not easy to push them down the throat. There were tears to swallow too.

This incident had relaxed Ram Khilawan's nerves to such an extent that he wanted to go home, for a brief moment, just to tell his grandmother that his masters treated him well. So that she too could sleep peacefully. But that was again impossible. He could go home only at Holi. And Holi was still too far. He had joined work immediately after Diwali. No matter how many times he counted the months between Diwali and Holi they never became less.

The discussions which took place between members of his family before he was sent to work kept echoing in his ears day and night. He wished he had a say in those discussions. If his grandmother had her way she would never have allowed him to be out of her sight. But the men of the family saw a lot of benefit in sending him to work.

'Ram Khilawan is too small even to look after himself,' his grandmother pointed out to Gayadeen, 'how do you think he'll be able to look after the headmaster's children? His kitchen? His house?'

'Amma, he will learn all that. He is an intelligent boy. And then, poor people's children take no time to pick up such duties,' Gayadeen answered.

'But he will make mistakes in the beginning which they will not overlook. I don't know how they will treat my little child.'

'I have had the occasion to watch them for some time. Remember, I told you Shiv Narain and I whitewashed their house and the school too. During that time we had ample opportunities to watch how they lived, what they thought and how they behaved. Amma, they seem to be good people.' Gayadeen was trying his best to satisfy his mother, 'I'll call Shiv Narain. You ask him yourself.'

'Shiv Narain,' Gayadeen called.

Shiv Narain was Gayadeen's older brother's eldest son. When the thunderstorm destroyed their harvest he started going with his uncle as an unskilled labourer to whitewash houses. Both of them were working for a man who had got a contract to whitewash and repair government property. 'Shiv Narain, tell your grandmother what you think of the headmaster and his family,' Gayadeen said, as soon as his nephew arrived.

'Daadi, they all seem to be God-fearing people. The day we were delayed, the headmaster asked us to stay back and sleep in the school. He asked his wife and sister to prepare dinner for us. Who does that for poor unskilled labour?' Shiv Narain said. But his grandmother was not convinced.

'My dear child,' she said to Shiv Narain, 'to look after the safety of two poor people one day and feed them is one thing, but to be kind to a child, who is completely at their mercy is another.'

'Amma, the thunderstorms this time were too ferocious and they occurred repeatedly. You are aware that they have left nothing. They destroyed not just the crop and the house, even our bull was killed,' Gayadeen explained.

'Yes, dear son, I understand. But thunderstorms never strike with the same ferocity every year. Next year things will be better, god willing.'

'And how do we feed so many mouths till then? If Ram Khilawan goes to work, at least he will get two meals a day and his wages will come as a great relief for us. Thirty rupees is no small amount. No one pays such a big amount to a small child for housework these days. Fact is, all three young people in that family are working; their two little children and old mother are alone the whole day. They need someone to be at home with them.' Gayadeen said all he could to satisfy his mother. He realised how much his mother loved her grandchildren. Ram Khilawan was particularly close to her, because she had brought him up. Ram Khilawan's mother had been severely ill for years after delivering him.

'And I would like to ask you just one question, not just you Gayadeen, you too Guniram and Nand Lal. Do you remember the great flood which had hit us years ago? That flood too, had left nothing. In fact the waters had taken away even the roof of our home. Your father had died long before the floods. I was alone. Did I then, even once, consider sending one of you to work for some family in the city?'

'No Amma you didn't,' all three replied at once, 'and we are thankful to you for that.'

A long silence followed. All three remembered how their mother had slogged for years thereafter at the local Zamindar's house and tolerated his insults. How helpless she was when he swallowed one whole bigha of her fertile land for a few rupees that she had borrowed from him. That was how her family was left with just the 15-biswa land which could never be enough for her growing family.

Shiv Narain picked up the conversation again, 'Daadi, the headmaster also says that if Ram Khilawan shows any inclination to studies, he will not leave him unlettered.'

'So you are planning to make Ram Khilawan a *baalister*?' This time his grandmother resorted to sarcasm.

'No Daadi, we are not so lucky, but if he learns to read a few books he may not have to fall back on hazardous jobs in times of emergency as we have had to,' Shiv Narain said.

'Amma climbing unstable bamboo ladders to whitewash at unthinkable heights is no pleasure. Every day death is staring you in the face and yet you go on because you have hunger also glaring at you with threatening eyes,' Gayadeen tried to explain the helplessness of an uneducated and unskilled man.

'I do understand every word of what you say, my child. But I don't trust these city people who employ little children of the poor. All they want from them is work. They do not realise that little children can't work as adults can. They beat them, they starve them and they think that they have bought slaves. My darling baby, my innocent little Ram Khilawan; he is so gentle. We have always nurtured him like a flower.' And she burst into sobs. Ram Khilawan, who was sitting by her side leaning against her and making desperate efforts to push back his tears, suddenly lost all control and sobbed putting his head in his grandmother's lap.

A heartrending shriek from the far end of the hut drew everyone's' attention to a woman who sat there with her two little children, her face covered with a *ghunghat*. She was Ram Khilawan's mother. No one sought her opinion for no one thought that she could also have one. The discussions ended on a sad note. Everyone dispersed with wet eyes and Ram Khilawan's initiation into working life was kept on hold for some time.

But for some time only. After another week when Gayadeen broached the subject, his mother replied with anger and annoyance, 'Do as you like.' For desperate Gayadeen that amounted to consent. And Ram Khilawan was taken to the headmaster's house to begin a new phase of life.

The attitude of the headmaster's mother towards him had no doubt put his mind in a peaceful mode but he could not get over his grandmother's restless eyes when he was leaving home. Those eyes followed him everywhere. They would not leave his side. At times he would become desperate to go home, just to tell his grandmother that his master and his family were kind to him, just to tell her that. He genuinely had no intentions of staying back at home. He didn't want to run away from his work. He knew that was not possible till Holi. And Holi was still too far. All he could do was to pray. He begged God to keep his grandmother healthy and alive while he was away. He wanted to see her hale and hearty when he went back home.

Then one day Ram Khilawan heard Ammaji tell her daughter-in-law to start giving lessons to him. 'But why?' the daughter-in-law asked.

'The boy will become more useful to us,' Ammaji said.

'That's what you think, Ammaji. The fact is that the boy will leave us the moment he becomes educated,' the daughter-in-law explained.

'You talk as though the boy will pass BA or MA after a few lessons at home. Never mind, I will ask my son to teach him.'

'As you please.' The daughter-in law left the room in a huff.

Ram Khilawan did not quite understand why Masterji's wife was against giving him lessons. But he didn't care either. By then, time had moved and Holi was just a couple of days away. Home was no longer a distant dream. His heart was full of joy at the thought of the seven days which he would spend with his dear grandmother. And lo and behold, the day arrived! His father was actually there, standing before him.

When he left with his father for his village he had a new set of clothes, ten gujhias in a polythene bag and three rupees in his little hands that were no longer soft but had turned rough with housework. Masterji, his mother and sister had each given him one rupee to buy sprinklers and colour to play Holi. Those presents were like a treasure for him. He was really excited at the idea of wearing new clothes. He didn't remember wearing new clothes ever, though his mother had told him that the first clothes he wore were new. His grandmother had saved money to get them for him, when he was born.

On the way, when they passed by a market Gayadeen suggested that they stop to buy colour and sprinklers, with the three rupees which his masters gave him. Ram Khilawan was not interested. He was thinking of his grandmother and mother in the worn out faded saris they were wearing when he left home. He wanted to buy new saris for them. The cheapest saris which were available could not be bought with the three rupees in his hands. His father was not willing to spend even a paisa from his wages. 'Beta,' Gayadeen said, 'all festivals, whether Holi or Diwali, are for children, not for elders. Bhagwan has been so kind to you. Look at the new clothes He has given you. Your mother and grandmother will be happier to see you in them than they would be, if they wore new clothes themselves. You have worked so hard, stayed away from home, we have all been weeping for you in your absence. If now I spend your hard earned money on such trifles like clothes it will amount to wasting your labour, my child.' Gayadeen tried his best to explain to his little son how much he appreciated his sacrifice. And the little son, who had always shown an incredible sense of responsibility for his age, said nothing in reply. He just swallowed some tears. Holi came and went but the new clothes which were given to Ram Khilawan, by his masters, remained in the polythene bag, untouched.

But the seven days were not totally sad for Ram Khilawan. He found happiness by giving those three rupees to his grandmother who was so delighted that she went boasting all over the village, singing her grandson's praise. At the end of it all she returned one rupee and eight annas out of the three to Ram Khilawan and said, 'Here, give this money to your mother. She should also benefit from the generosity of her son.' And when Ram Khilawan gave the money to his mother he sensed another whiff of happiness envelop his heart.

He spent those seven days sitting with his grandmother for hours listening to stories of her life. He got to know a lot about her dreams and wishes. Most were unfulfilled ones. And one wish of hers clung to his heart and soul. This was a desire of hers which could still be fulfilled and Ram Khilawan swore to himself that, come what may, he would not let it fall on that sad heap of unfulfilled wishes. He had heard his grandmother, with rapt attention, narrating the incident about her going, when she was a young bride, with her husband to a place called Jhusi near Allahabad to attend a wedding in his uncle's family. On their way back the bus gave way right on the Jhusi Bridge. They had to wait there for several hours. The passengers spent the time watching the Ganges from the bridge. But the sight before them was no pleasure to watch; it was horrific and gruesome. Heaps and heaps of human bodies had accumulated against the pillars of the Jhusi Bridge, naked bodies with hairless heads shining in the rising sun as though painted grey. An elderly passenger said that they were bodies of poor people for whom cremation was out of reach. That scene was imprinted on the young girl's mind, for all times to come. It left just one lingering wish in her heart that her last rites be performed on the banks of the Ganges. But the rites should include a proper cremation which would reduce her body to ashes. And those ashes be put first in an urn and then only, slipped into the holy waters.

'But I also know,' she said with a sigh, 'that I am wishing for the moon. For poor people like us, even to get new cloth for a *kafan*, is unthinkable. Maunds and maunds of wood, pure ghee and endless other things are required for a cremation. Who will be able to buy all that paraphernalia, for me? From where will the money come for that, and for paying the *pandas*? Hey Bhagwan!'

'Daadi, I will get all that for you. I will continue to work hard and with honesty. I will not rest till I have collected all the money required. But Daadi, please don't die.' And he dissolved into sobs. The grandmother hugged her little grandson and both wept like never before.

And the seven days came to an end. It was time for Ram Khilawan to leave home again. Everyone in the family including the women accompanied him with heavy hearts walking along till the end of the village. From there his father put him on the carrier of his cycle to drop him at Masterji's house. This time when he resumed his work it was again, as though, he had left home for the first time. From the first day he started counting the days left for Raksha Bandhan. He realised it was exactly as far away as Holi was from Diwali.

It was more difficult settling down this time than it was last time. The days were no problem because he had a lot to do. But nights were too long and had become frightening. Sleep distanced itself from his eyes. The terrible scene from the Jhusi Bridge which his grandmother had seen when she was young would appear before them, in a more horrendous avatar, each time he closed his eyes and tried to sleep. And he would get up with a start and resolve to himself that he would not let his daadi's body pile up on that heap of grey bodies. But how will he save all that money for a proper cremation? His father would never spare even a rupee from his wages. For him the loan he had taken from the *mahajan*, with its ever-soaring interest, had to be returned first. Nothing was more urgent than that. The ten year old could see no solution before him for this massive problem which he had willingly placed on his tender shoulders. In a state of despair all he could do was to weep.

In the modest two-roomed apartment which the masterji's family occupied it was not difficult to make out that someone was weeping. Ammaji guessed immediately that it was Ram Khilawan.

She got up and came out into the veranda where Ram Khilawan slept.

'Ram Khilawan, what is the matter, are you not well?' she asked.

'I am alright,' he said.

'Then, what is the matter, why are you crying?' she asked.

'I am not crying,' he said, rather embarrassed.

'Okay. Come here,' she said with affection.

'No Ammaji, you go to sleep, I am alright.'

'Come here, come to me, immediately.' She repeated with authority. And he came trying his best to hide his tears.

'Has anyone beaten you?'

'No Ammaji.'

'Has anyone said anything nasty to you?' She wanted to know what was troubling him.

'No,' he repeated.

'Are you missing home?' He broke into sobs.

'I know my child you have just come back from home. Was everyone alright at home? Your grandmother too?' And he broke into another bout of sobs, so uncontrollable this time that Ammaji had to give him some water and caress his head.

After some time when he was a bit relaxed, he told Ammaji about his grandmother's wish to be cremated on the banks of the Gangaji.

'So that is what is troubling you?' she said feeling relieved that she had found the reason.

'Yes Ammaji, I want to fulfil this desire of hers. She has had a very hard life, even harder than that of my father or mother. She has done such a lot for all of us and never wished anything for herself. But where will all the money come from? Everyone says cremation is very expensive.' Ram Khilawan suddenly felt that he could tell Ammaji everything.

'Don't worry Ram Khilawan, I'll make some arrangements if the need arises,' Ammaji said.

Ram Khilawan did not express joy at the offer. He wondered where she would get such a lot of money from. 'Ammaji, won't that be difficult for you,' he said and added, 'you don't have a job.'

'My children will help me arrange for the money,' she said casually.

'It will take me a long time to return the entire amount. I will work for you free till the whole amount is paid. You won't mind that?' Ram Khilawan wanted to make sure.

'No, no, you won't have to pay back. We'll bear the expenses. It is *punya* to arrange for the last rites of a poor person.' Ammaji said with a saintly look on her face.

'But Ammaji my grandmother always taught us not to beg, even if we are starving. I will somehow return the amount.' Ram Khilawan said innocently and looked up at Ammaji hoping that she will be pleased at his reply. But she was not. Her face suddenly acquired a harsh expression.

'I made an offer which few would make. If you don't want to accept, it is your lookout. Go, go and sleep now,' Ammaji said rather severely which surprised Ram Khilawan, but he immediately turned towards the rags which made his bed.

In the morning he got up as usual and started sweeping the floor. Just then Ammaji entered the house with her daughter and daughter-in-law with puja *thalis* in their hands. They were returning from the temple. Seeing Ram Khilawan, she addressed him saying, 'Haughty little brat that's what he is.' Then she told her children the previous night's story. Her daughter-in-law immediately reacted, 'Those who are born low remain humble only so far as they are starving. As soon as they get enough food to eat they imagine that they have become equal to those who feed them.' The daughter said nothing but her body language indicated that she didn't approve of what her sister-in-law said. Masterji, who was also there, rebuked his wife, 'Who is feeding him, may I know?'

'We,' she answered.

Masterji's face became red with anger at his wife's comment. 'Don't be under any such illusion. He is earning his bread; we are doing him no favour.' Then looking at his mother he said, 'Ammaji, you should be happy that the boy, despite his age, despite his poverty, has so much self respect.'

'I realise that beta, I was surprised that the kid had the audacity to turn down my offer which I had made out of sheer affection for him. Now let's forget it. I'll make your breakfast otherwise you'll be late for school.' Ammaji wanted to put an end to the matter. But her daughter-in-law could never forget the harsh words her husband had spoken to her and all because of Ram Khilawan. She became determined to teach him a lesson.

Ammaji's attitude became normal with Ram Khilawan though the matter regarding the cremation was never discussed again. And Masterji became friendlier towards him. He bought a book for him and started giving him lessons. In the meanwhile, his sister had realised that Ram Khilawan was very good with his hands. She allowed him to sit with her when she was making dolls, paper flowers and other such things. Such handwork was part of the school curriculum which was entrusted to her. Ram Khilawan picked up that art faster than her expectations though he was slower with his books. And then one day, Ram Khilawan asked Masterji to allow him to learn cycling.

'Masterji if you allow me to learn to cycle I will take hot food for all of you every day at lunch time.' And sure enough Ram Khilawan was soon an expert cyclist too. By then, time had moved on to another Diwali when Ram Khilawan had completed full two years serving Masterji's family. This time settling down after coming back from home was not so difficult. In fact he looked forward to learning new things from his masters. He was slowly accepting his masters' home as his own, when he suddenly realised that there was truth in what his grandmother said, about city people ill-treating little children whom they hire for housework.

On a Sunday morning, not very long after he came back from home, he heard Masterji's wife shouting. Apparently there was some money missing from her purse. Masterji had gone out to give tuition to a student in a village some distance from Unnao, and Didiji had gone to Lucknow to meet someone who promised to get the increment of pay due to her, which was not being released. Only Bahuji and Ammaji were at home. 'Why don't you count the money again,' Ammaji told her.

'Ammaji, I have counted the money in my purse several times, I think you count the money which I gave you for house expenses,' she said. Ammaji went running to her room, unlocked her tin box where she had kept the money and ran back to her after counting the money that was given to her. 'I don't have a paisa more than what you said you gave me,' she said almost breathlessly.

'I knew you don't have it, because I know where it is. It is with your favourite Ram Khilawan,' her daughter-in-law shouted.

'Bahu, Ram Khilawan is not a thief. He is with us for two long years. Have you ever lost anything during this time?' Ammaji asked with anger.

'No I haven't, but I know these children are taught by their parents to start clearing up the house after they have won over the confidence of the masters. You don't know them, Ammaji, so you keep quiet. I know how to take out my five rupee note from him,' the daughter-in-law said firmly and pounced on Ram Khilawan who was standing in the veranda transfixed to the floor in a state of shock. She gave him a few tight slaps and banged his head against the wall a couple of times. The boy fell unconscious on the floor before Ammaji could intervene.

'What have you done just for five rupees, you wicked woman! What should I do now? Hey Bhagwan!' But before panic could overtake her senses, she called for a rickshaw and took Ram Khilawan to the local hospital. She had to call a man from outside to help her lift the boy and put him in the rickshaw. When people, who had collected at her door asked her how the boy got hurt, she told them that he was flying a kite on the roof and he fell down! She gave the same statement to the doctors in the hospital. But the hospital informed the police nevertheless. Before the police too Ammaji repeated the same statement.

The police was contacted by yet another person about the incident. He was the father of a seven year old student, whom Masterji's wife, who was also a teacher at the government school had, some months earlier, stripped and beaten in her class for not doing his homework. He was unable to get his report lodged then, because the Police Inspector was indebted to Masterji for giving free tuitions to his son. The little student's father was waiting, since then, for an opportunity to teach the woman a lesson, for disgracing and beating his child. This time the man was heard. The Police Station had a new Inspector.

The Inspector arrived at Masterji's house with a lady constable to interrogate his wife even before Masterji and Ammaji could rush to their house to save the situation. By then Masterji's wife had already told the Inspector that she had found a five rupee note missing from her salary which was kept in the purse. She said that she had *very gently* asked Ram Khilawan if he had seen it anywhere and the boy started banging his own head against the wall and fell unconscious. The Inspector took her statement in writing too. Her statement obviously clashed with that of her mother-in-law. By late afternoon while the police was still in the house, Masterji's sister came back from Lucknow. When she saw the confusion in the house, she rushed to her brother's wife and said, 'How could you have forgotten that you gave me a five rupee note to buy lace from Lucknow for the children's dresses. You even said that Lucknow has the best lace and *gota*!'

People from the neighbourhood also spoke to the police. They bore testimony to the fact that Ram Khilawan was a very gentle child, was never seen playing or even holding a kite in his hand leave alone climbing up the roof to fly it. One young man even told the police that he had peeped inside the house when he heard the screaming and shouting and saw Ammaji's daughter-in-law banging the child's head mercilessly against the wall. All evidence had gone against Bahuji. The police was preparing to put her in the lockup, when the local MLA intervened and persuaded them to wait till Ram Khilawan gained consciousness.

A constable was sent to Ram Khilawan's village to call his father. The poor father arrived with his nephew Shiv Narain and was almost mad with grief when he saw his son in that condition. He became a pale shadow of his former self in the few days that he was there. All he said during that time was, that he was a cruel father to have sent his son to work at that tender age. That he was a disobedient son, not to have paid heed to his own mother, who went on begging him not to send the child to work.

But luckily Ram Khilawan opened his eyes on the fourth day. He got up and sat on the hospital bed when he saw his father and hugged him. 'Take me home Bappa, take me home, don't leave me here again.' But the doctors kept him in the hospital for another ten days before discharging him. Even the police was allowed to talk to him only on the last day, though all he told the Inspector was that he didn't remember how he got hurt. His father had instructed him not to say anything against any member of the family. The poor man was too scared for his son. And the police, for some reason, didn't insist that the child should try to remember.

The father refused to take the money which Masterji tried to give him when he was leaving for home with his son. 'I am taking back my son alive, what wealth can be greater than him,' he said and walked straight towards the bus station without looking back. And when they sat in the bus Ram Khilawan said, 'Promise me, Bappa, you won't tell Daadi anything, she will be very unhappy.' Gayadeen hugged his son and said, 'I'll make a more sacred promise, my dear child. I'll never send you away from home again. Even if I'm not able to feed you, even if I am not able to pay back my loans, I'll always have you and all children of my family, in front of my eyes. Forgive me Ram Khilawan. Forgive me my child. I have taken away two precious years of your innocent childhood.' All three wept inconsolably.

Everyone was happy at home to see Ram Khilawan hale and hearty and so were neighbours and relatives. People were told that he had met with an accident when he was going to give lunch to his master. No one was happier than his grandmother. When Gayadeen told her that Ram Khilawan was not going back to work, anymore, she fasted for three days to thank God for granting her request.

For one month Ram Khilawan did not work. He was advised total rest. But after that he started worrying. He had to work, he thought, to fulfil his grandmother's wish. He must also help his father to clear the loan which was yet not fully paid. For some time he worked in the fields. But he soon realised that too many people of his family were already working on the 15-biswa land which the family owned. His efforts were not going to yield anything more. He realised that he should do something else, to add to the income of the family. And he did.

He persuaded his father to lend him a few rupees. With that money he bought sheets of coloured paper and left over cloth from the village tailor. That was the raw material with which he made bouquets of artificial flowers and stuffed dolls. There were initial failures. But drops of success soon sprinkled on his efforts when he started going to the neighbouring villages and the village fairs to sell his wares. He realised that he earned a little more than what he earned at Masterji's. But all that he earned was spent to keep the kitchen fire burning. He could save nothing. But he was happy to be with his family as was everyone else.

And one day his grandmother said to Gayadeen when her other sons and daughters-in-law were also present. 'Have you noticed that ever since Ram Khilawan has come back home and started selling flowers, none of us have ever missed a meal, by the grace of God.' Everyone agreed with her. And she continued, 'When children are happy and kept with the family by the elders only then prosperity enters the house.' Though an expression of guilt spread on Gayadeen's face he said, 'Forgive me Amma, never again will I disobey you.' And he looked with gratitude at his son. But Ram Khilawan was lost in his own thoughts. He was worried that he had not so far been able to save the money to keep the promise he had made to his grandmother.

His work picked up when Shiv Narain brought a contractor who decorated marriage mandaps with artificial flowers. Ram Khilawan started supplying the decorations to him. His income, no doubt, doubled, but not in proportion to the hard work which went into it. In fact his mother and younger brother who were also very good with their hands had joined in to help him make the paper flowers. But he could still not save as much as he planned to. The home expenses were rising with the prices going up and then there was his sister's wedding. But at least, during this time everyone enjoyed good health in the family, which was no small mercy. He never forgot to thank God for that.

He was sixteen when his grandmother's health started deteriorating. He had saved five hundred rupees by then. He spent lavishly on her medicine and treatment. He wanted her to recover and to spend her old age without pain. She did recover and remained absolutely fit and happy for many months. And then one morning, when her family least expected, she was gone. She died in her sleep peacefully and apparently without pain. At that time Ram Khilawan had three hundred rupees with him, which he had saved many months ago, and into which he would never dig, but could not add any more to it either. Ram Khilawan told the family elders about his grandmother's wish regarding her cremation on the banks of the Ganga and his promise to her. They were all with him and wanted to help him, but at the time of her death all that the whole family had, was just fifty rupees. Ram Khilawan consulted a couple of people who knew how much money was required for a dignified cremation. They assured him that three hundred rupees were enough for that. But at least a hundred and fifty rupees more would be needed for taking the body to the banks of Gangaji. No hearse car would take less than that. Gayadeen offered to take a loan from the *mahajan*.

'He will willingly give the money, because now the earlier loan has been paid,' Gayadeen said. But Ram Khilawan did not agree.

'No Bappa, Daadi would not have liked to go on borrowed shoulders and that was not my promise to her either. And don't forget Bappa, what trauma we went through to pay back your earlier loan and interest.' All the elders put their heads together but could find no solution because a hearse car could not be hired without money and Gangaji was too far for people to take the body on their shoulders.

Ram Khilawan was not one to give up. He had got more love from his grandmother than what he got even from his parents. For him she was no ordinary woman. To fulfil her last wish was all that he wanted. He had left no stone unturned to save enough money for her cremation. So what if there was not enough money to carry the body till Ganga Ghat in a motorised vehicle. 'I am a good cyclist,' he thought, 'Why can't I carry the body on the carrier of my cycle and reach it to Ganga Ghat?'

Ram Khilawan's determination bore fruit. The *arthi* was taken on people's shoulders till the end of the village. Many villagers joined the funeral procession; some had also come from the neighbouring villages. When they reached the road to Kanpur the shrouded body complete with strings of fresh flowers was placed horizontally on the carrier of the sole cycle which the family possessed and tied firmly to it with a wooden plank underneath the body. Ram Khilawan rode the cycle with his grandmother's *arthi*. He volunteered to reach it till Ganga Ghat in Kanpur. Gayadeen, his brothers, all their male children and two of their cousins, were to take the bus to Ganga Ghat.

The rest of the villagers returned to their homes, except two who had cycles. Those two were unskilled labourers who were going to work at a place a couple of kilometres away. Till there they would give Ram Khilawan Company. But only till there. After they left, Ram Khilawan was to be on his own. He was not worried. He was sure to reach the body to the banks of the Ganga safely and fulfil his grandmother's wish. Gayadeen, however, was not sure. 'My child, how will you go so far with the body, all by yourself? My heart is bleeding; once again I have placed too much responsibility on your shoulders.' He had made all possible efforts to borrow a cycle so that Shiv Narain could accompany Ram Khilawan and share with him the burden of cycling with the *arthi*. But the few people who had cycles in their village had to go to long distances for work. No one could afford to miss a day's wages. Gayadeen was restless. Looking at his brothers, he repeated, 'He is all alone, how will he go so far?'

Ram Khilawan had already started riding the cycle. And Gayadeen heard Ram Khilawan, shout back with confidence, 'Gangaji is not far, Bappa.' But the truth was that Gangaji was too far for someone riding a cycle with a shrouded corpse, on a hot June day, with no one else to share the burden. Ram Khilawan's fellow villagers, left three kilometres later, when they reached their destination. Other cyclists on the highway made sympathetic enquiries and moved on. It was several hours when Ram Khilawan had only completed twenty kilometres. He was half dead with fatigue. Around that time a Police Inspector who was patrolling the area on a motorcycle with a constable on his pillion, intercepted him. Ram Khilawan riding his cycle, with a shrouded body on his carrier, was a strange sight for anyone. Obviously the Police Inspector looked at him with suspicion.

He asked Ram Khilawan many questions, saw the face of the dead woman and looked convinced of the truth. But he did not let Ram Khilawan proceed. He offered to carry Ram Khilawan and the body on his motor cycle for the rest of the journey. For Ram Khilawan, that was too risky an offer, coming from a policeman. When the Inspector said that unknown people also offer to lend their shoulders to a passing *arthi* and relatives willingly accept the offer, two fellow cyclists, who had stopped by to see what was happening, decided to intervene. They asked Ram Khilawan to accept the offer.

'Beta,' one said, 'Darogaji is not offering you any money; he only wants to help you carry the body.' But Ram Khilawan took time to believe that a policeman can have such good intentions!

'My child, you look hopelessly tired and you have only covered half the distance. Please let me help you with the other half. My constable will bring your cycle by bus to Ganga Ghat, I assure you,' the Inspector pleaded. Ram Khilawan took God's name and did as he was asked and in twenty minutes time the Inspector reached him and the body, to the turning to Ganga Ghat. Gayadeen and Shiv Narain were waiting with the rest of the family at the turning point, with a cot, to carry the body to the river front. Ram Khilawan was more than relieved to see them. The Police Inspector went with the procession to

Ganga Ghat and attended the cremation which was done, in an extremely dignified manner, just as Ram Khilawan wanted. By then the constable had also reached with the cycle.

Ram Khilawan lit the funeral pyre of his dear grandmother. Gayadeen and his brothers felt that, even if it meant a break from tradition, their mother would have wanted it that way. When the body was totally burnt, the ashes were put in an urn. Ram Khilawan lifted the urn carrying her ashes, touched it to his eyes, and lowered the vessel, gently, into the holy waters of the Ganga. As he stood watching the urn sail away on the water bed, there was no sign of fatigue in his bones; there was no memory left of that humiliation and trauma inflicted upon him at Masterji's house. No traces of a deprived childhood lingered in his eyes. He felt like a strong prince who had conquered the world.

Let Me Have a Love Affair

Prashant had done his schooling from his village school. But there was no college there and so his father sent him to Lucknow where he stayed with his uncle and did his Intermediate and BA from a college established by two brothers who belonged to a family from Prashant's village. He had come to Lucknow several times earlier during summer holidays. Once he had gone, with his cousin, to see a Hindi film. He had enjoyed the film thoroughly. Prashant was very excited to be in the city. His father wanted him to complete his post graduation from Lucknow University. That meant he would be visiting his village only once in a while. He preferred to be in Lucknow with his cousins rather than in the dreary old village. He longed to make his home in a big city.

Prashant was right. Lucknow was a lot more fun because his cousins were a fun- loving lot. They had nothing to worry about except their studies. Two of them were still in school. The eldest, who was older than him, had completed his studies and was preparing for Competitive Examinations because that was the only way to get good government jobs. But somehow they always found time for Hindi films. This was despite their parents' restrictions. They saw at least one film per week. And Prashant was always with them. He loved watching films. He too got addicted to them.

What impressed him most about the films was that the hero and heroine never got married without having a thoroughly good romance. They would saunter around hand in hand, sing songs in beautiful gardens, near gurgling rivulets, cascading waterfalls. Even if they did not get married to each other, at least they had had their share of fun. If the film was a tragedy and the hero or the heroine got married to someone else at the insistence of their parent or parents, that other person would also not be all that bad, at least to look at. Those three hours in the cinema hall were really enjoyable and a great stress-buster. He always came back, after seeing a picture, in a curious state of mind, wanting to know how one fell in love, what one felt while being in love. He just wanted to be in love. He wanted to go around with a girl just as the heroes in films did. And that would be the time he would never think of his wife, back home in his village. Never once did he imagine he could have a romance with her. Thinking of her on such occasions made him irritated.

'Why were my parents in such a hurry to get me married? My uncle in Lucknow never got his sons married,' Prashant would grumble to himself. 'And they call her beautiful, just because she is fair and rich and has five brothers, all doing well. Didn't they see her two protruding teeth? They scare me.' Prashant wished he also had found a wife for himself, like the film heroes do, after falling in love. There were times when he was irritated and depressed. There were times when he felt quite rebellious too.

Prashant's parents had got him married when he was in his Tenth Class. For them that was something quite normal. That was the age when they and their relatives had tied the knot. Arranged marriages at a young age was the system followed by everyone in the village. There was nothing unusual about it.

It was worse for Prashant when he started going to the University. His irritation knew no bounds. The girls in the University and even in his class looked so different from his wife. They spoke so well, they dressed so well. Some of them looked like the film heroines and yet they were so well behaved.

'Only if my parents were not in so much of a hurry to get me married, maybe, I could have married one of these girls!' Prashant would think and curse his luck. How strange he felt when at times he noticed some boys talking to girls in a very casual manner, 'They must have been brought up in cities and for sure they couldn't be married like me,' he would think. He was so conscious of the fact that he was a married man and by then also a father of a two-year old son that he became quite reserved with the other boys too. Though once in a while he would walk down with some of them to the library or to the Registrar Office and often chatted with them in quite a friendly manner, he never disclosed to anyone that he was married.

This way a year passed. At the beginning of the second year which was his final year for completing his post graduation, he was standing in a queue to submit a form at a window outside the Registrar's office. A girl came rushing in and requested the boy before him in the queue to let her stand in front of him. 'Please may I? I am in a mad rush. Got to submit this form and am running late for class,' the girl requested without any hesitation or inhibition.

'What makes you think I'm not in a hurry,' the boy retorted, in a harsh voice.

Immediately Prashant offered to give her his place and she accepted with profuse thanks. That left Prashant in a kind of a shock. He was really surprised at himself. Till now he had never ever started a conversation with a girl. He was indeed quite pleased with his act of chivalry. The girl's happy reaction took him to another world altogether and raised his self esteem. After submitting her form the girl ran towards her class but didn't forget to turn her smiling face towards him for another round of thanks. Prashant's day was made.

The whole day he spent thinking about the girl. Where would he find her? He had no clue. How he wished he had asked what exactly she was doing. That would have made it easier for him to meet her again. Now it was impossible to locate her, he was sure. Surprisingly for him, Lady Luck chose to be on his side. He did spot her again and above all, in his own Department! She was in the First Year MA. And Prashant who thought he was an introvert with no self confidence, took no time in reaching out to her. 'So you are also doing Mathematics,' he said to her when she was standing with a group of girls. The girl turned around and looked at him for a minute, 'Oh ... you, gave me your turn at the window na?' Perhaps his face had not quite registered in her mind. But that did not deter Prashant from giving his complete introduction. 'I am also doing MA in Mathematics. I'm in the Second Year. My name is Prashant Ku....' The girls she was standing around with burst into a giggle; even she looked embarrassed. 'See you later, got a class to attend,' the girl said, indifferently and moved straight towards her class. But Prashant was unfazed. In fact he appeared quite satisfied, having met her and having introduced himself to her.

He had three consecutive lectures after that, but his mind was involved in planning his next move, thinking out one strategy after another. There was no sign of her for the next three days. On the fourth day he saw her in the Library. She was standing near the catalogue cabinet. He walked stealthily and stood near her as though he also just happened to be there to consult the catalogue. Finding someone standing so close, she turned towards him. This time she had no problem in recognising him.

'Oh it's you,' she said with obvious relief, 'perhaps you can help me.' Prashant became nervous. He knew he was not too good with books. He waited with bated breath to know what she wanted. The lecturer had emphasised the importance of a book for the subject he taught in her class that day. She had written the name of the author in her note book, but couldn't find it. This time again, Lady Luck decided to stand by Prashant. He knew the name of the author and the book! And also knew that the library had several copies.

'Oh thanks a lot, you're great, you've saved such a lot of my time. Now I can sit in the reading room for an hour and try to understand the subject,' she said.

'Why do you have to sit here? Why can't you issue it and keep it with you for some time?' he asked.

'My Library Card is still not ready. The Librarian will give it to me only by Monday,' she explained.

'I'll get it issued on my card,' he offered.

What more could she want.

This was a very big development for Prashant. That was the day he got to know that she was called Aparna Devi and lived in the Ladies' Hostel since her father was posted out of Lucknow.

The impression Aparna got about Prashant was that he was a very helpful person, simple and utterly harmless. She spared him no thought beyond that. All that she kept in mind was that she had a library book issued on his card, which she should return as soon as possible. For Prashant it was much more. He felt that his days of bad luck were over.

Prashant was floating in a heavenly atmosphere. He felt that he was in love but also wanted to know what it was to be loved by a girl. He would not be happy till Aparna started having the same feelings for him. To be in love was not enough, that was only one-sided, and one-sided love was no love. He would not be satisfied till he was also loved in the same way. Joy would not be his. So he continued to exercise his mind, making plans and building strategies to attract her towards him. He made himself his pleasantest best, gave a lot of attention to his dress and behaviour, offered her his help at the least opportunity.

And finally Aparna noticed that she was getting a lot of attention from him. In the beginning she tried to ignore it. She had never lived away from her parents and had been brought up as a very duty conscious child. And those were different times. Undue mixing of girls and boys was frowned upon. But Prashant did not give up. Initially she resisted his compliments and praise, but she was a young girl after all. She gradually started getting convinced that he really loved her. She felt a certain softness entering her heart for him, and noticed herself drifting towards him. And soon the time came when she was desperately in love with him. She was happy in the University only when she knew he was around. Back in the hostel it was a minute to minute wait for the next day.

During winter holidays she went home and explained the whole situation to her parents who were willing to give their nod after meeting him and his parents. It was then that she realised that Prashant had not proposed marriage. She couldn't wait to get back to him to broach the subject. She was sure that would be the first thing on Prashant's mind and when she gets back he'll greet her with the proposal. And so he did. Prashant talked of marriage in an indirect manner.

As they sat in the Lucknow University Milk Bar sipping a delicious strawberry milkshake, Prashant said, 'Aparna do you realise there are just a little over two months left for our final exams?'

'Of course I do and I also realise that it's time I started preparing for the exams,' Aparna replied.

'For me these will be my last two months in this University. You know what I will be doing during the summer holidays? I'll be preparing for the State Bank exams for Probationary Officers. You know this way I can even reach the highest position in the State Bank.' He said it all in one breath.

'So you plan to be a big officer?'Aparna teased.

'I have no other option. To qualify as your husband I can't be anything lesser,' he said and looked at her for a reaction.

She only blushed. She had heard what she wanted to hear from him. She didn't think there was any need to tell him that her parents wanted to meet him and his parents, before giving their nod. She was sure that he had enough perseverance and intelligence to get through the exam. For him to meet her parents only thereafter would be the best thing. Her parents would never refuse someone with high prospects.

On another occasion, just before the Preparation leave, while they sat in the Milk Bar for a little respite, Aparna, who was dreading not the Exams as much as she was dreading those two long months of the summer holidays when she would be away from Prashant, made a suggestion. 'Why don't I also fill up the forms for the State Bank exams? It would be better for me to be busy with something. Oh God, otherwise I'll miss you to death.'

Prashant was thrilled to hear that admission of love coming from Aparna's lips, but he did not want her to venture into those areas where he had some plans.

'That would be a great idea, nothing like both of us in the same service. Life would move so smoothly then, both at home and in the office,' he said, then paused, as if he was thinking. After sometime he said, 'But Aparna, I think it would be better if you completed your MA before you tried your hand at any of the competitions. ONE – because you'll be better prepared and TWO – You'll have an option. An MA in Mathematics is a solid degree for a teaching job.'

'Yeah, you're right. I was only trying to find something to keep myself busy.'

But she filled the SBI form and sent it on time, for she knew she needed to do something to save herself from a breakdown. And she informed him that she had done so.

After that, the hectic preparations followed by the examinations gave them little opportunity to meet each other. And then the time came for the separate journeys to their respective homes with promises to write to each other without fail. Aparna wrote letter after letter but all that she got in reply was a single typed inland letter in which he said he was missing her and that he was very busy preparing for the SBI exam.

Prashant was indeed preparing for his exam but his mind was on something else. He was now looking for an escape route from the love affair which he had woven for himself. It did taste well so long as it was in progress. He soon realised that he was not acting in a film where the story could be turned and twisted according to the writer's whims. It was life. And life is not run by one's desires. Life is much more than singing and dancing near cascading waterfalls. And above all even in the films the heroes and heroines see happy endings only when they are not cheating each other. From day one Prashant only wanted to have the feel of a love affair. And after that he thought he would just shout 'Cut' and 'The End' would follow.

The results of the MA examinations may have surprised him, for it was a poor second division which he got, a performance which could not take him far. But the results of the SBI competition came as a relief. He had qualified. What surprised him was that Aparna Devi had also qualified! Aparna noticed that he was not very comfortable after the SBI results. When the call letters came he had cheered up again. Both of them had their training schedules in different cities. Anyway they parted on a happy note.

There was one other boy, Ajai Shankar, from his class, who had qualified along with them. Ajai Shankar had his training schedule with Prashant in the same city. In fact they shared the hostel room. A few months later a young man came to meet Prashant. He had gone somewhere. Ajai was there. He asked him to wait till Prashant came back and made him a cup of tea. While talking to the person Ajai realised that he was related to Prashant.

'How are you related to Prashant?' Ajai asked.

'Prashant is my sister's husband,' the visitor replied. Ajai was shocked for he knew Prashant as a bachelor. Prashant had told everyone in the university that he was not married. Ajai also knew, like everyone else, that he was going around with Aparna Devi. People in the Department believed with good jobs in hand, they would soon get married.

'When did Prashant get married?' Ajai enquired.

'He has been married for seven years. He has a four year old son!' the visitor replied.

Soon Prashant arrived. His face turned white on seeing the guest. Ajai did not disclose to Prashant that he had had any conversation with the visitor. But at the first opportunity he wrote a letter to Aparna informing her of what he had learnt. He felt it was his duty to disclose the news to her as soon as possible.

Aparna was devastated. She was all by herself, in a strange city. And yet she did not want to believe, what Ajai had written to her, until she had heard it from Prashant's lips. She booked a ticket to the city where Prashant was being trained. She found him in the Trainees' Common Room. She requested him to come out with her for some time. She made him sit in the taxi she had hired. Confused, Prashant followed her into the taxi. After the cab had travelled a couple of kilometres Aparna turned towards him and asked, 'Prashant are you married?'

'I am a very unhappy person ...' Prashant stammered, making a desperate effort to clear himself of his guilt.

'I'm asking you a very simple question. And I want a straight answer, in a monosyllable. Are you married? "Yes" or "No". Answer me, right now.' She spoke with authority.

'Yes,' he answered.

She asked the driver to stop the taxi, opened the door and said, 'Get out.' Prashant did not have the courage to resist. He slipped out like a thief and found himself in the midst of the traffic jam which was caused by the sudden stopping of the vehicle. And then the taxi moved ahead. And so did Aparna's life, in a painfully slow motion.

Aparna did find a partner for herself and had a family too, but time took too long to heal the wounds inflicted by a Hindi cinema buff who used her as a guinea pig to experiment in life what he saw on celluloid.

Trial and Punishment

It was a large house in which I lived during my Allahabad posting. There was a larger stretch of land attached to it on which our office was built. On the days when my work delayed me, I would not go out, but walk around my bungalow. On one such day I saw an urchin, a skinny boy, with some semblance of clothes on his bony frame walking with great confidence on the space between the office and my house. When I asked who he was, he told me, without getting nervous, that he worked in the teashop at the gate.

'But what are you doing here,' I asked.

'I brought tea for the Sahib,' he said pointing in the direction of the Control Room, 'I bring tea every evening.' I realised that the persons posted in the Control Room must be ordering tea and refreshments from the roadside shops, because they were on duty for long hours, in fact for the whole night. The Office Canteen would close with the office. My first instinct was to instruct the officer on duty to ensure that the teashop boys did not loiter around in the office premises. But on second thought, I didn't. Instead, I asked the boy his name and invited him to eat something at my place. He was quick to give his name. 'Irfan,' he said, but refused to eat. 'I am full. I don't feel like eating,' he said. I felt pained to hear that. Hunger was writ large on his face. He was obviously hesitant. Maybe, he was afraid of going into the house. And I didn't want to let him go without giving him a meal. After much persuasion he sat down in the veranda to oblige! He ate well. It appeared that the poor boy was really hungry. He left with a big smile on his face, which left me smiling too for some time.

Days later Vandana, my Personal Assistant, casually mentioned that a boy who works in a teashop on the roadside wanted to work for me. 'Where did you meet him?' I enquired.

'He came to me,' she said. I was rather surprised. I did not expect such enterprise from that urchin, nor did I expect him to know the protocols of an office.

'That would be very good. Tell the teashop owner that I want to employ him,' I told her.

The lady came back to me and reported that the owner of the shop had refused to relieve the boy. I was very surprised; the teashop was exactly on our gate. He knew we could get him thrown out. The shop was thriving because of the location and he had other boys working for him too. He could easily dispense with one. 'How could he afford to refuse,' I wondered. 'Madam, the shop owner said that he had purchased the boy from his brother for sixty rupees, so he had every right on him,' Vandana said in a very matter of fact manner. I was shocked; more surprised at Vandana for not reacting with anger when she heard about the purchase and sale of a human child.

'Vandana, do you realise that human trafficking is illegal. It is a crime. That teashop owner can be sent to jail. How could he dare to boast fearlessly about buying a child and claim his rights on the movements of that child? Vandana, I am more shocked at your lack of reaction! You stood there with a straight face and kept silent. Do you realise that you are working in a law enforcing organisation?' I could not control my anger.

'Sorry Madam,' she said and left the room, disappearing into the long dark corridor. She was back within no time. She informed me that the teashop fellow fell at her feet and begged her not to inform the police and said the boy could go wherever he wanted. 'Madam he wanted to touch your feet and beg your forgiveness. He said he will never buy a child again!' The little boy had accompanied Vandana into my room. He stood there by her side, with a smile broader than the one he had flashed on the day when he left after having his dinner at my place.

'There is no need for that rascal to come anywhere near me, least of all, to touch my feet,' I said harshly and left it at that, deciding to deal with him later. It was already quite late so I got up and went home along with the boy.

A good bath and a change of clothes gave the boy another face and another structure. And then after he had had a good meal I decided to ask him a few questions about his family and home. The first thing I wanted was to restore him to his parents. What surprised me was that he kept going back on his answers though he stuck to the name of his father and that of his village. He did not give the correct information about his mother. He started off by saying 'she is alive,' then suddenly he would say, 'No she is dead.' That wavering filled my mind with a lot of doubts. Am I doing the correct thing by keeping the boy in my house? Is he genuine? I wondered.

'But when I first met you, you said your father was dead and your mother was alive,' I reminded him.

'I meant my step-mother was alive and if you send me there she'll beat me. You keep me here with you. I'll work for you,' he begged.

'Alright,' I said, 'you stay here. Don't worry.' He did not appear eager to go back to his village at all. And I was afraid that if I insisted, he might run away and get into greater trouble. I sent a trusted person, the following day, to his village which was just an hour away from Allahabad, with the address which he had given.

The information the boy gave turned out to be correct, except what he said about his mother. His real mother was alive though slightly crazy and had difficulty in walking due to some defect in her legs. The neighbours told the gentleman who had gone there to make enquiries, that her stepson had carried away and sold everything which she had, including sewing machines which her husband, who was a tailor, had left at the time of his death. They told him that he also took away her son and said he was going to get him a job. One man from the neighbourhood informed, 'When the little boy did not return for a long time, the poor mother asked him where her son was. He said he sold him, as brazenly as that. Since then the mother lost whatever was left of her mind.'

The gentleman came and reported the matter to me and said, 'The mother's condition is pathetic. We must reunite the son with her without any delay.' But Irfan was reluctant to go. He said his stepbrother would not spare him. He would snatch him away again and take him elsewhere and sell him again. He was afraid that his mother was too weak to protect him. He also said that though the neighbours sent food to his mother when she was hungry, they never intervened when his stepbrother came and caused havoc. I realised that was the reason why he was not willing to give the correct information about his mother; so that he may not be sent back. He may have guessed that I will send him to his mother if he tells me that she was alive. He was sure he was not safe there.

But after staying at my place for a few days he himself offered to go to see his mother. Perhaps he was convinced that I would never abandon him and would definitely protect him from the likes of his stepbrother and the teashop owner. 'Madam I'll go to see my mother, she must be very sad. She must be thinking I'm lost or dead. But please send the Sahib with me and tell him to bring me back the same day.'

'But if you come back the same day you'll make your mother unhappy.'

'No,' he said, 'I'll convince her that now I am free and working with very kind people.' I realised that Irfan did want to see his mother but didn't want to stay in his house for long. He was still not sure whether he'd be safe there.

I told him then that there was an office of the department in his very town also and there were many people who worked there. They would ensure his safety. I said, all I could, to erase the fear entrenched in his heart. Irfan went finally, stayed for some days, and came back looking very cheerful.

On his return I sent Irfan to my parents in Lucknow where he was extremely happy. After being with them for sometime he disclosed a lot of terrifying acts of Chaudhry, the teashop owner, which he had remained tight-lipped about at Allahabad. He never spoke voluntarily about him even there; he had to be coaxed into it.

There was a big white spot on his left foot. On being asked what it was, he said he had got burnt.

'How?' my mother asked.

'I dropped tea on it by mistake.'

One day the driver came to my mother and informed that there was a similar mark on his back and on his upper arm. Without any further ado my mother consulted a doctor to find out whether he had any pigmentation problem. The doctor was very sure that the boy had got burnt.

'How did you drop tea on your back? Someone else must have done it. Come on, tell us who did it. Don't be afraid.' Both my parents coaxed him gently. At last he opened up.

'Chaudhry would wake us up by pouring boiling water on us, if ever we overslept. He wanted us to get up at dawn and start work at the shop even if we had gone to sleep late the night before,' Irfan said. His face looked fear-struck perhaps at the memory of it. And then he told them that once Chaudhry poured too much boiling water on Chunnu, another boy, who worked with him. The boy never recovered from the burns and died a painful death. My parents were shocked.

When I heard Chunnu's story, I felt that I was duty bound to get Chaudhry's shop removed from our office gate, and get police action initiated against him.

In the meanwhile Irfan continued to work at my parents' house in Lucknow. My mother said he was quick to learn. After two years, when I was posted to Lucknow, I realised Irfan could cook and bake well and even handle small dinner parties, all by himself. And soon he became an indispensible part of our household. He was very good with his hands. One didn't have to call a plumber, electrician or even a carpenter. He could easily mend small defects of electrical gadgets. Even an air-conditioner was not beyond him. But Irfan had his problems. He was far from disciplined. He didn't eat his food until he sat in front of the television. When sent out on an errand, he would disappear at times for the whole day and be found playing video games in some nearby shop. He would avoid having a bath, washing his clothes, even his hands and face at times. My brother once stood outside the bathroom to ensure that he had taken a bath. My parents' indulgence was doing no good. My father saw to it that no one was over strict with him. He always said that with time, as he grew a little older, he would himself shed all those bad habits. And he did.

My parents were, in their own way, training and grooming Irfan very effectively. While I was, trying in vain, to see that Chaudhry got due punishment for treating poor children cruelly. The police, no doubt, booked a case against him, but one never heard of any progress. I did manage to get him and his shop removed from our office gate, but in no time it reappeared on the opposite pavement which was attached to the Inter-city bus station. That was an even better location for a teashop. He became still more prosperous. His prosperity was at its height when I was transferred out of Allahabad.

My transfer left me happy because I was going to Lucknow to set up a new office. But the fact, that I could do nothing about getting Chaudhry punished, weighed heavily upon my mind. I would often grumble about it before my parents.

Once my father said to me, 'Your duty is to see that things improve, nothing more than that.'

'But things didn't improve, despite my efforts,' I said, disappointment rife in my voice.

'So what? You contributed your mite, didn't you?' he said.

'Maybe I didn't put in as much effort as was required,' I said, after thinking where I could have gone wrong.

'Required for what?'

'Required to punish Chaudhry,' I answered.

'My dear child, trial and punishment should be left in the hands of God. He can handle that better,' father said and left for his room. My mind definitely felt lighter after that. I forgot about Chaudhry and the punishment that he deserved.

All this while, Irfan was not only handling household work, but also going to a nearby school. When he was eighteen he was given a temporary Class IV job in my office. In another two years after he had passed his Eighth Class he became a permanent Sepoy. It was a joy to see him in the office in his khaki uniform.

Many years later Irfan was posted to Allahabad. He was already Head Hawaldar by then. When he went to report for work at the office, he stood at the gate for a long time, waiting for the flood of memories to recede. And then he looked for the familiar teashop. It was missing. He did not see it on the opposite pavement either. But an old man in rags sat on the ground with his head bent. Irfan went up to him to find out about the teashop. 'Baba, there used to be a teashop here, why is it closed today?'

The old man looked up with expressionless eyes and said, 'Which tea shop? I don't know. I haven't eaten for two days.'

As the man looked up, Irfan realised he was Chaudhry. He put a big note in his outstretched hands and walked straight into the office.

Where Did the Delicacies Come From?

She was obviously, given a name by her parents, but no one knew what it was. They called her Amma while addressing her, but when talking about her referred to her as Ghausia ki Amma (Ghausia's mother). She was a widow who lived in a large house next to ours. It was not the whole house that her family occupied but just one third of it, on the first floor. That was all they needed. There were two more totally independent portions of the house which she had rented out. A good old woman, she was. Very helpful and warm. Our two families became friends in the late forties. When friendship grew, some bricks were removed from the wall that separated our houses, to create a window-cum-door, which made walking into each other's houses easier. The generations that followed never lost track of each other.

When the friendship began, Ghausia's mother had been a widow for thirteen years. Her husband died somewhere in the mid 1930s. She lived in that house with her daughter Ghausia and her two sons Abdurrehman and Fazlurrehman and also a granddaughter, Saira, who was older than her three children. She had one other daughter who was married and lived in Banaras; that was what Varanasi was called then. Saira's mother was her eldest child. She died shortly after Saira's birth. Ghausia's father died later, after moving into that house. He fought a long battle with all kinds of diseases before succumbing to them.

Though he was a little above fifty at the time of his death, both his sons and daughter were still too young. There was no one who could take over his business in leather which was quite a prosperous one. It slipped into the hands of an employee and Ghausia's mother could do nothing about it. She had a year or two of a very harrowing time. Her finances improved only when she rented out two portions of her house.

Ghausia's mother would often sit with us and talk of various incidents in her life, some normal, some funny, some strange too! She had a way of making her conversation interesting. People flocked round her to hear her talk. But she would seldom talk about the period in her life during which she had financial problems. Only once she spoke about it to my mother. It was a strange incident, pertaining to that period, which she narrated.

'My husband had left us no small wealth. I have no reason to complain,' she began, 'There was this big house and not less than a seer of gold jewellery but no cash whatsoever. Whatever cash we had, was spent on his illness. He had been ailing for a long time. To keep the fire in my kitchen burning, I was only left with the option of either selling the house or the jewellery and I was determined not to part with either.'

Ghausia's mother went on to explain why she was determined to hold on to both her jewellery and her house. She had the responsibility of raising three children of her own, the eldest was seven and the youngest three. Then there was Saira, her granddaughter, who was only eight. Some education at least had to be given to her sons. And to marry two girls was bound to cost her a lot. Selling the house was unthinkable. Where would she find shelter for so many little children? She had to weigh matters from all angles before she decided to sell either of these two things.

Her cash lasted a few months and then there was darkness all around. One day she found nothing in the kitchen that she could cook. She managed to scrape some rice from a container which she boiled in the afternoon and handed a ladle each to the children and to Ahmadi the orphan girl who looked after the children during better days. Ghausia's mother had sent away her two servants, immediately after her husband's death, but Ahmadi had stayed behind because she had no place to go.

That one ladle of rice was not enough for the children. In no time they were hungry again. They started crying and shouting. By evening they were restless. Ghausia's mother was herself on the verge of a breakdown. She begged her children to go to sleep.

'My dear little ones go to sleep, when you get up you will get Pulao and Zarda to eat.' She mentioned the names of those delicacies just to quieten them for some time.

'Pulao and Zarda?' seven year old Abdurrehman said with disbelief, 'You promise?'

'I Promise,' their mother answered, and then uttered under her breath, 'Ya Allah ... help me.'

'But there is no rice and sugar in the kitchen and no meat. How will you cook the Pulao and Zarda?' Six year old Ghausia knew what was there in the kitchen and also what was needed to make Pulao and Zarda!

'When all of you are sleeping I will send Ahmadi to get all I need to make the dishes,' Her mother said very convincingly.

'But Amma, Ahmadi does not know where meat is sold,' Ghausia said.

'Amma I know Ishaaq's shop! It is very near our house. I went there once when you sent Ghulam Nabi to buy meat. Let me go with Ahmadi, I'll show her the shop.' Abdurrehman became so eager to help, that their mother had to change her tone.

'Look, I had said if you go off to sleep, only then you will get Pulao and Zarda to eat.' Ghausia's mother said sternly, fully realising that sleep refuses to come on an empty stomach. But all four lay down on their cots and closed their eyes, to keep their part of the promise.

Ghausia's mother left her poor obedient children struggling to get sleep and went into the kitchen, hoping to find something to cook. But all the containers were empty. There was no wood either. Even if she had found something, there was no possibility of cooking it.

She came out of the kitchen, determined *not to let her children starve any more. She was convinced that the time had* come for her to start selling her jewellery. But she had never gone to a jeweller's shop. When her husband was alive a jeweller used to come to her house, very often, with his wares and she would buy whatever she wanted from him. She never thought of asking him where his shop was or where he lived. Her husband knew him and often went to his shop. The only other person who knew the jeweller and his shop was Ghulam Nabi, her trusted servant whom she had dismissed because she couldn't afford to give him his wages. Luckily he lived with his wife in the vicinity of her house.

'Hurry up Ahmadi, go and call Ghulam Nabi,' and as Ahmadi left for Ghulam Nabi's house, Ghausia's mother headed for the storeroom where she kept her boxes and valuables. She took out a ring which was very light in weight, from her jewellery box and decided to start her selling spree with the lightest item. By then Ahmadi was back, with the news that Ghulam Nabi had gone out for some work. He was to come back by late evening. Ghausia's mother was very upset. Without Ghulam Nabi there was no possibility of reaching the jeweller's shop. All that she could think of was that her children were starving. If Ghulam Nabi came back after the jeweller's shop had closed there was no likelihood of getting any food till the next day. She prayed to Allah to send Ghulam Nabi back in time.

Suddenly there was a knock on the main door. She got up with a start and screamed, 'Ahmadi, there's someone at the door. Go fast and open it. I think Ghulam Nabi has come.'

Ahmadi rushed down the staircase to open the door. In a few minutes she was back with two big dishes placed on a tray.

'A gentleman brought this tray of food. It is a gift from a neighbour who is celebrating the birth of a son,' Ahmadi explained.

'But didn't you ask which neighbour? Go, run and find out, he must still be there, waiting for the dishes.' But the man who had given the tray to Ahmadi was nowhere. She ran down the whole length of the road till the crossing but found no trace of the man who had handed her the tray of food. She came back to be told by Ghausia's mother that the two dishes contained Pulao and Zarda! The children were woken up to a regular feast. Even after Ghausia's mother and Ahmadi had eaten, there was plenty left over for breakfast.

'But who could be the neighbour?' Ghausia's mother was curious to know.

'Don't worry Amma, the gentleman will come back to get his dishes, we'll find out then,' Ahmadi said.

'I am sure he will. Copper dishes are so expensive,' Ghausia's mother said and then looking at the dishes more attentively, she added, 'Don't they look somewhat like the dishes of my copper dinner set?'

'Pots and Pans in most homes look the same, Amma,' Ahmadi said.

'We must remember to send the newborn baby a good present. Because of him we got a feast when we needed it most.' Ghausia's mother was happy beyond words.

'Amma, it was like a miracle,' Ahmadi couldn't contain herself either.

'So it was! We have only Allah to thank for it, He saved us from starvation and allowed me to keep my word with my children.' Ghausia's mother was all praise for her Creator.

'How strange Amma! You promised the children Pulao and Zarda and it was exactly those two delicacies that our neighbour sent us and right at the time when the children were about to get up from their sleep!' Ahmadi pinched herself to ensure that she was not dreaming.

The following morning the leftovers of the Pulao and Zarda served as a very satisfying breakfast for all. After breakfast the children were playing around in the courtyard when there was a loud knock on the main door. Ahmadi ran down the staircase with the dishes in her hands, absolutely sure that the man who brought the tasty delicacies was back to claim his utensils. But it was Ghulam Nabi standing at the door with another gentleman.

'I want to meet Amma,' he said.

Ahmadi took him upstairs. Ghulam Nabi had actually brought a tenant for the two vacant portions of Amma's house. The tenant paid ₹ 40/ as one month's advance for the two portions. And that was the end of Ghausia's mother's financial woes though the rent she got from her tenant could just pay for a very frugal lifestyle. But at least she was sure that the next meal was coming even if it was just daal roti and that there was a roof over their heads. Above all, the tenant and his wife turned out to be good people and of great help to Ghausia's mother, throughout the period when her children were growing up.

But no one ever came back to get the two dishes and the tray in which the Pulao and Zarda had been delivered to their doorstep. Ghausia's mother and Ahmadi had made all sorts of enquiries. But they got no reports about any celebrations in the Mohalla on that day or the day before for the birth of a son. Finally they gave up. The two dishes and the tray kept standing on the top shelf of their utensil rack in the kitchen reminding them of the Pulao and Zarda which arrived at their doorstep at an unthinkably opportune moment.

And then, one day Ahmadi decided to do a stocktaking of the pots and pans and other utensils. Actually Ghausia's mother had found a groom for her and was about to get her married in a week's time. Ahmadi, who had total charge of the kitchen, wanted to show what was where, to Ghausia's mother before leaving for her husband's home. While sorting out the utensils she found two oblong dishes missing from the dinner set which the family used with great pride only when special guests were invited for a meal. There hadn't been any such occasion after the passing away of the master of the house. So the dinner set was never taken out from its wooden case. Ahmadi was obviously distraught.

She ran to Ghausia's mother and told her, 'There are two oblong dishes missing from your dinner set Amma.'

'But the dinner set was inside the wooden case. We never took it out of the box,' Ghausia's mother said.

Ahmadi started weeping. 'Amma I don't know anything. I have opened the case for the first time.'

'Did I say anything, my child? Calm down,' Ghausia's mother said gently.

Ghulam Nabi, who had been called by Ghausia's mother to lend a helping hand, was also there. He counted the items of the copper dinner set and then looked around in other parts of the kitchen and in the store room where the wooden case was kept. Then his eyes rested on the utensil rack in the kitchen. He picked up the two copper dishes from the top shelf of the rack and said to Ahmadi, 'Here are the two dishes you were creating such a fuss about.'

'These are not ours,' Ahmadi said emphatically.

'Someone brought us some eatables in these dishes,' Ghausia's mother explained.

Ghulam Nabi took back the dishes and turned them upside down. 'See, Haji Sahib's name is written on it and on this one too.' he said and showed the engraved name on both the dishes to Ghausia's mother and to Ahmadi. But both of them were illiterate. Ghausia's mother called her children and asked them to read. Each one read aloud by turns, 'Haji Sharfuddin.'

'How can that be,' Ghausia's mother said with disbelief.

'That's not possible,' said Ahmadi, who appeared to be in a state of shock.

'Why can't it be possible? Remember Amma, Haji sahib used to get his name engraved on all utensils. I was with him when this dinner set was purchased. He left the dinner set with the shopkeeper and told me to bring it after his name was engraved on every item.'

Of course Ghausia's mother remembered that her husband, who had been for pilgrimage to Mecca Sharif and whom everyone addressed as Haji Sahib after he came back, not only got his name engraved on utensils but also got it embroidered on his clothes and bed sheets. But how could his name be on those dishes which came from somewhere else! She was in a daze, she just stood there speechless, holding Ahmadi's hand.

At last Ahmadi spoke, 'There is a tray there too, see if Haji's Sahib's name is engraved on it also.' The name was there. Ghulam Nabi said, 'Two trays, one big and one small, were a part of the copper dinner set. This is the smaller one, I just saw the bigger one inside the wooden case.' And looking at Ghausia's mother and Ahmadi standing there as though in a dream he couldn't help saying, 'Amma what has happened to both of you?' Ghulam Nabi was genuinely concerned. 'You said that someone brought some eatables in these dishes. Alright, tell me, who brought them?'

'An angel.' Ghausia's mother said and walked out of the kitchen and Ahmadi walked out behind her, both still in a daze.

Virginity Lost ... So What

Kumkum's parents had at last found a boy for her, who was, like her, a doctor.

And who like her, had specialised in ophthalmology. From all angles he was suitable. But, surprisingly, Kumkum refused to marry him.

'What is it that you find wanting in him?' her mother asked.

'Nothing at all,' she said. 'Amma I don't want to marry, yet.'

'Yet? What do you mean by yet? You've already allowed a lot of time to go by, my dear child. It would be foolish to wait any longer. Remember, you are not getting any younger.'

Kumkum's mother got up in a huff and walked straight into her husband's study. 'I don't know what to do with this child.'

'Which child, who are you talking about?' her husband asked.

'I'm talking about Kumkum and you know that. I think, it's time you took over charge concerning Kumkum's marriage. I can't fathom what exactly she wants in her man.'

'I firmly believe that the charge should remain with you,' the father replied. 'You can handle it better. Girls are generally reluctant to open up to their fathers. Have some patience, she'll tell you what she wants. It's possible that, at the moment she herself, doesn't know what she's looking for in her husband.' Then after a little while he suddenly said, as though a bright idea had occurred to him, 'Why don't we take Rita's help? Both of them are childhood friends, very close to each other. And Rita is an intelligent girl, she'll very easily find out what Kumkum wants.'

Rita was Kumkum's best friend. They had studied in the same school since nursery. Both did medicine, though from different medical colleges. Another reason for their being so close to each other was that they lived in the same neighbourhood.

There were no secrets between them. The idea appealed to Kumkum's mother. So the entire matter concerning Kumkum and her suitors was, ultimately, entrusted to Rita.

'Kumkum, Aunty tells me that you're being difficult,' Rita began the work entrusted to her in right earnest.

'I am not. Amma doesn't understand,' Kumkum replied.

'What doesn't Amma understand, Kumkum?' Rita then posed a more direct question, 'Do you want to marry the man your mother has found for you or you don't?'

'I do not.'

'You know Kumkum, when you refuse a proposal for marriage you must always give clear reasons for doing so. What is it that you find wrong with him?' Rita was not going to let her friend get away with vague answers.

'I find nothing wrong with him.'

'And yet you don't what to marry him? Kumkum, there must be something wrong with you.' Rita was really surprised. Suddenly, she remarked, 'Hey, I hope you are not still in love with that Calcutta fellow? If you are, than you are crazy.'

'Not at all,' Kumkum said indignantly, 'I am indifferent to Himanshu now! I don't give a damn about him.' Kumkum tried to convey to her friend how much she detested the guy. She explained at length how embarrassed and ashamed she was, now, to admit even to herself, that she was at one time, in love with him. She couldn't believe anymore that she had broken down emotionally when the affair fizzled out.

'I may have had a long relationship with Himanshu but today I'm happy that he did not marry me. A man who could so successfully fake a relationship for so long was not worth marrying. He was a con man.' Kumkum paused and then continued, 'And yet Rita, my refusal to marry the gentleman Amma has found for me, is only because of that relationship.'

'Strange!' Rita said, 'What do you mean?'

Kumkum narrated the relationship she had with Himanshu. Step by step she recalled how it started and developed over the years when both of them were classmates at the Lucknow Medical College. They knew each other from the first year, but it was in the third year that they became friends. Their fondness for each other grew with every day that passed. And soon that emotion developed into a deep love on both their parts, or so she believed. There was nothing that Himanshu didn't do or say to make Kumkum feel that she meant the world to him. His actions and words, his little notes and gifts created a happy world around her and made her feel that no one in the universe could love another more than he loved her. And when love becomes so intense it does not remain hidden from others' eyes.

Soon their affair became the talking point of the campus. Some students would talk about it with exaggeration, others would criticise it, but everyone took a lot of interest in what was happening between them. Many even envied them. Their affair was no secret even from the teachers and the Principal. Himanshu and Kumkum were going around like a couple. Once even the Principal called them and told them to concentrate more on their studies. He also asked them as to what their future plans were about each other. Both said they were planning to get married. In fact Himanshu said he wanted to get married to her as soon as they completed their MBBS. They even informed the Principal that they would not wait to complete their internship. The Principal had left it at that.

But after completion of the five year medical course, it was Himanshu who suggested that they do their internship before getting married. Surprisingly, during the internship, Himanshu seldom mentioned marriage; though earlier it was he who was more vocal about marriage and their life together. He would talk about their future, as though in a dream, making it appear so cool, so tender and so beautiful. Now it was Kumkum who would broach the subject and Himanshu would once in a while, reluctantly participate in the conversation. Sometimes he would say that they'll first see where they get seats for Post-graduation and then think of marriage.

Then, one day, Himanshu mentioned that his mother was ill and that he was going to Calcutta to see her. On his return from Calcutta Himanshu told Kumkum, much to her dismay, that he had discussed his marriage plans with his parents and neither of them was willing to have a daughter-in-law who was not from their part of India. They had insisted that Himanshu should marry a Bengali girl. But seeing Kumkum upset, he immediately made light of the situation by telling her that he was sure he would ultimately be successful in persuading his parents to agree to their marriage.

About her own parents, Kumkum was always sure that they would not have any objections. She had already told them about Himanshu and of her intention to marry him. They had welcomed her decision and expressed their eagerness to meet Himanshu as early as possible. She promised to bring him over to them after their internship.

After the internship was over, Kumkum suggested to Himanshu that he accompany her to her home in Allahabad and leave for Calcutta from there, after meeting her parents. But Himanshu did not agree. He told her that it was best, that he reaches home, and talks to his parents about their marriage, without wasting any time. Kumkum saw nothing wrong with that. She went to see him off at Lucknow Railway station as he boarded the Punjab Mail for Calcutta. But that was the last she saw of Himanshu.

She spoke to him several times on the phone. Though each time, all he said was, that he had not been able to talk to his parents because his mother was having heart trouble and if he broached the subject, she would possibly get a heart attack.

Gradually he stopped taking her calls. So long as she could hear his voice on the phone, doubt or fear did not enter her heart. But when he started avoiding her calls the world turned upside down for her. She became restless. She could not concentrate. All that she wanted was her relationship with Himanshu to get back on track. Everything else was unimportant, even her career was pushed to the back burner. It was at this time that she got a seat for post graduation in Lady Hardinge Medical College in Delhi. But even that brought her no joy. She was in no state of mind to join. Her priority was to be in Calcutta first, so that she could know the fate of her marriage. She boarded an eastward bound train and reached Howrah Railway station.

Himanshu's address was in her diary. She headed straight for his house. It was his mother who answered the doorbell. At the very doorstep, Kumkum was informed by the lady that her son had got married and that his wife was a very senior officer's daughter. When Kumkum insisted on meeting Himanshu, his mother sternly told her that that was not possible. But she allowed Kumkum to talk to him on the phone.

Kumkum asked Himanshu whether he was married. She heard his voice, saying with no apparent regret, 'Yes I am. I couldn't convince my parents, I'm sorry.' And then Kumkum heard the phone disconnect. With that all remnants of hope also disconnected from her existence. She was left with no alternative but to return to Howrah Railway station. She boarded the earliest train and sobbed her way back to Allahabad. This was no small tragedy. The betrayal left Kumkum shattered. She took years to recover. But recover she did, thanks to her parents' positivity and love and Rita's support.

The Kumkum now sitting before Rita was a stronger woman, open and honest, her past having left no traces of bitterness on her personality …

'What do you mean Kumkum, by saying that it is the relationship of yours with that spineless creature which is preventing you to marry this man who your mother has chosen?' Rita could not understand Kumkum's reasoning, since she had accepted that Himanshu did not matter.

'Rita, I've to be totally honest with the man I'm going to marry.' Kumkum explained.

'Who's stopping you,' Rita said. After a pause she added, 'But you are under no obligation to tell him about what happened between you and Himanshu.'

'I am. Our affair was not limited to exchange of sweet nothings. We were actually living together. I've lost my virginity,' Kumkum uttered the words with great difficulty.

'So what?' Rita took no time to react.

'Rita!' Kumkum screamed with horror.

'How are you so sure, Kumkum, that your suitor's virginity is intact? Do you have any way of finding that out?' Rita was quick to rebut. And Kumkum just stared at Rita, not knowing what to say. After a little while she said, 'Rita, there won't be many men, in India, who would say "so what!" if they are told that the woman they are considering for marriage has lost her virginity.'

'So, why tell them?'

'Because that's the right thing to do.' Kumkum was convinced not to go ahead with her marriage without sharing her past with her suitor.

'Well if you insist, your mother and father will fix a meeting. The two of you can be all by yourselves.'

***

And so Kumkum and her suitor met in the living room of her own house. Her parents and Rita kept away from the room, but remained within the house. The conversation started on a cheerful note but very soon the suitor could be heard shouting. The parents and Rita were taken aback. They decided that it was time for them to come closer to the Living Room. They came and stood, all attention, behind the curtain of the door which opened into the parents' bedroom.

'Are you not ashamed to tell me that you're not a virgin, madam?'

'Sir, it was the correct thing to do. Since you'd come with the intention of marrying me, I have to reveal this fact to you.'

'You've indeed been very kind. Thank you. Now do me another favour, permit me to leave.' The man's voice was dripping with sarcasm.

'As you wish,' Kumkum said, and her 'suitor' got up with a jerk and walked out saying, 'Even the air of this house is polluted.'

This was not the last time that Kumkum heard unsavoury things about herself. She came face to face with many other suitors. She was adamant to 'tell all' despite Rita's advice against it and ended up seeing each one walk indignantly away after calling her names.

***

In the meanwhile, Rita had to leave India, because she got married to someone who was settled abroad. Kumkum and Rita met years later when Rita came on a visit to India. She was pleasantly surprised to find Kumkum happily married to a very successful surgeon. She had two lovely children and she was getting along well with her career too.

'So, at last dear Kumkum, you found someone who said "so what" to your disclosure?' Rita asked.

'No, I didn't find any such person,' Kumkum said honestly and added with a smile, 'I followed your advice, at last!'

The Magic Wand

There are times when you don't know what you are so happy about. You need someone else to tell you the reason. I was not just happy, I was in a state of ecstasy. An experience of thrill overpowered my mind and body. It was Nidra, my room-mate, who remarked when we came back from the music room, one day, 'Do you realise, dear girl, that you have fallen for that new boy, that one, who, for some reason, joined the Academy almost a week late.' I made no denials, no excuses like other girls would. For a moment I looked at her with surprise and then my thoughts went back to the music room where some probationers were sitting around Jyoti who was singing a song. Another probationer was accompanying her on the tabla. Must have been a melodious rendering by her, for the music master was giving her approving glances and the probationers were all attention, except the new one who was concentrating on teasing me and cracking jokes and I was enjoying every bit of his teasing and trying to tease him back. Nidra had watched all that.

I gave no answer and Nidra did not insist. Both of us were getting late for dinner. Punctuality had to be adhered to at the

Mussoorie Academy. We concentrated on changing our dress. But Nidra had sure made me aware of a reality. It was a fact that I had been swept off my feet by the new probationer.

I had met him just before dinner, the day he arrived. That was the time when probationers sat in the lounge and mingled with each other. They were in a state of excitement till then, because they had also arrived just a week before and were eager to know each other.

Normally I used to walk from the Ladies' Block with some probationer, but that day I entered the lounge all by myself. I think I had made an early entry. It was a very cold evening though one week of March had gone by. I had wrapped myself well in woollens and covered my head with a royal blue dupatta. At the far end of the lounge, near the radiogram, on a beautiful old fashioned three-seater sat a service mate of mine along with another person. They stood up and smiled when they saw a lady enter. I headed towards them and sat down on the seat they offered. The gentleman from my Service, whom I had met several times in the last one week, introduced the newcomer to me as an old friend of his. They were together at St. Stephens in Delhi. He too had joined the same Service as us, but had resigned because he had been selected for a Public Sector Undertaking where his salary was to be much higher than ours. He was likely to stay on with us, for perhaps another month, till his resignation was accepted.

Normally I would go around the lounge and join different groups to get to know other batchmates. But on that day, somehow, I continued to sit with the two of them. The newcomer mentioned some friends from my hometown who were with him in school and asked me if I knew them. I knew some. Most of the conversation was formal till it was time for dinner. Incidentally we also sat down for dinner together. There his jokes and teasing had started, evoking giggles from me. I found myself quite relaxed in his company because there were many common things between us. We came from the same part of India, went to the same type of schools and colleges. The only difference was that we called our Creator by a different name. I was indeed happy thereafter but I took no notice of it, for apparently all probationers were happy at the Academy.

It was a place which filled one with a lot of gaiety than any college or university campus does, for like a college the Academy had classes, games, sports and theatre but there were no tensions of having to pass examinations. You had overcome all that and above all, had come there after fulfilling your ambition of landing a prestigious government job. The mountains and beautiful weather mingled a lot of romance in the air. With a great job in hand, all that the young people thought of, in the Mussoorie Academy, was to find a life partner.

There were many *eligibles* around, scores and scores, to choose from. But eligibility of a partner was hardly on my mind. There was something splendid happening around me and I couldn't see beyond that. I just wanted to live in that splendour. I did not want to look beyond it even for a brief moment. The world around me had become magical. Who had created that magic I did not know, till Nidra told me. Strange indeed are human minds. And stranger are their reactions.

After classes most boys and some girls would go to the games field, some would busy themselves in the Music Room. I was good at neither but I hung around in both the places, sometimes to watch friends, at times to try my hand at table tennis or badminton, end up as a total flop and become a cause for humour for the probationer who stood around watching my game with mock interest. My day would be made, if the jokes were cracked, at my expense, by the newcomer. One day he played a game of table tennis with me and believe it or not, to the great applause of the amused spectators, allowed me to win.

But I was also good at something. And a chance to excel came my way too. The Fine Arts Society decided to put up a One-act play with just three actors, two males and one female. Vikram, from my service, was the director. He also played the husband's role. The newcomer and I played the other two roles. After a month's hectic rehearsals the play turned out to be a thumping success. The Academy photographer took many photographs. Surprisingly the newcomer who otherwise called me *bandaria* (female monkey) as a reaction to my calling him *bandar* (monkey), did not make fun of my pictures. He looked approvingly at them, particularly at the one where I was all by myself. I heard him tell Vikram that I looked like a geisha girl.

The rehearsal days were the happiest ones. Like all happy days, they flew with the wind and left behind the inevitable realisation that the newcomer's resignation had been accepted. He had to leave within four days two of which were Saturday and Sunday!

But before that the whole Academy went gaga over our play and wherever we went we were showered with congratulations. At least that kept my mind away, for some time, from his impending departure. But only for some time. At the Academy I had never been alone with him. We had got into a group. And it was as a group, that we went about and interacted. Four people from the group were from Delhi. Though leave in the Academy was not easy to get, our Delhi friends managed to get station leave for Saturday and Sunday and left for Delhi. I was alone and wondered how I would meet him before he left.

Despite all the teasing and joking and my apparent confidence I was too self-conscious to approach him. 'What will he say?' I thought with nervousness. Supposing he says 'No' or makes an excuse, it will be so embarrassing. All negative thoughts kept flooding my mind. I was restless. I was not prepared to let him go without meeting me, for he was going away forever. My heart was beyond my control, but my mind was pulling me back from doing anything that I would regret later. Finally I decided to walk down to the dining room for breakfast, hoping to find him there. And sure enough, he was there at the door of the Dining Room.

'I thought you won't have breakfast today,' he said with the usual teasing expression in his voice.

'Why?'

'Because your friends aren't here. What is food when friends are not around,' he quipped.

'Come on,' I said, and sat down at the table with him, hoping that breakfast would never end.

And while at breakfast he suggested, much to my heart's delight, 'Why don't we go out for lunch today and for a film?' My heart leaped. And before I could control it, he said, 'Oh I forgot! You are from Lucknow, too *nazuk* for two programs in a day.'

By then I had gathered the confidence to banter, 'You are right about my *nazakat*. Let's go for Lunch today and a film tomorrow.'

'Absolutely fine,' he answered. I thought I had made my dream come true. To spend parts of both days with him was all I wanted. At that moment, but only at that, it slipped my mind that after those two days, I may never see him again.

We walked down from the Academy and had lunch at a quaint restaurant at the far end of the Mall. He asked me whether I would like to have lunch at the Whispering Windows. I expressed my preference for the other end of the Mall for obvious reasons. I wanted our walk together to last longer. At lunch and during the long walk from the Academy and back, both of us were quite reserved, our conversation was no doubt, interspersed by an occasional joke and of course teasing. But I noticed we talked more freely, when others were present. I was very conscious of myself. But I did venture to say, 'It is a wonder how you could think of leaving a career like ours.'

'Yes,' he replied, and with an emphasis on 'now' he went on. '*Now* I wonder too. And I also know that a rolling stone gathers no moss.' I couldn't understand what he meant, by the latter half of the sentence.

It was already dark by the time we reached the Academy for it was a fairly long walk. The following day was the film and that was the last day. The early part of the day was spent by him on 'Thank you' calls to the Director and other staff members. My day began in the afternoon when we headed for the matinee show of a Hindi film. The conversation during the film was about the actors and their acting, but of course punctuated by a joke here and some teasing there. But that day, even his jokes were weighed down by a peculiar heaviness. There was a certain sadness in the air.

On our return to the Academy, he escorted me back to the Ladies' Block and while saying a goodbye gave me a small cartoon figure made of black rubber like material, which looked like a monkey and said, 'This is for you. Doesn't it look like me?'

'Yes it does,' I said with a forced giggle and turned around, to run up the stairs of the Ladies Block. He turned in the opposite direction to walk down to the Men's Block. Up in the veranda just outside my suite I stood framed in the window, with a sinking heart, to watch him go for the last time. In the backdrop of the deodars and greying mountains his tall lanky figure appeared to be dragging itself with an effort. I continued to watch him till he disappeared behind the Central Hall, leaving the giant deodars behind him.

What followed was a never-ending restlessness. I was happy that there was no one in my suite. Nidra had not returned. The third girl who lived in the single room of the suite was also not there. Perhaps she was chatting with some girls in another suite. To be alone was all I wanted. I felt like a severely wounded animal who expects succour from none. My agony could only be handled by my own resources. That I knew full well. I did not even wait for Time's Healing Touch. Above all I did not want anyone to look at me with pity. Though there was not much possibility of anyone knowing, except Nidra, about the inclination of my heart. I became more of an extrovert, more chirpy. I made my giggles and laughter appear heartier. That was the remedy I had prescribed for myself. Nidra, in the meanwhile, had got involved herself and had started planning for her future. Her attention was diverted from me. And that suited me, though my strategy was not all that easy. To hide one's pain successfully from others is more painful than the pain.

But some relief came when a 'Thinking of You' card arrived from him and a month later a several-paged letter. Of course there were no promises to meet again in the letter. But the fact that he was thinking of me and could sit down to write to me was enough. It was countless times that I read that card and that letter. And each time the reading gave me the same satisfaction which the first reading had done. He continued to write throughout the two years of probation, with gaps of at least four months between letters. But my repeated readings showered upon me some kind of a refreshing relief and filled me with a strange belief that he did not get lost forever, behind the Central Hall, on that last day when I watched him go from the window of the Ladies' Block. With every reading, I became surer, that even if he does not walk back from behind those mountains and the giant deodars, I would find him, one day, standing before me, in flesh and blood. And I did.

After the probation I had a short posting in Lucknow. He dropped in at my office. Later in the year he met me at Nidra's house in Delhi when she called some friends over for dinner. It was there that he gave me a big wooden monkey and said, 'That's me. Isn't he?' And I giggled, this time genuinely. The next evening I was travelling back to Lucknow. He came to the Railway Station to see me off. I was ecstatic.

Then came my long posting to Delhi, where he was also posted. He would come very often to see me in my Hostel on his way back home from office and sit around in the beautiful lawn to talk to me. Though I never heard what I longed to hear most from him. In his presence, I felt the same joy as I would feel in the Academy days.

But gradually he reduced the frequency of his visits. I continued to take the initiative of inviting him, though the frequency never went up. When he did come he radiated the same warmth and a kind of affection. And for me it would be a world of magic once again. But there was restraint in him and an unusual self control in his jokes and teasing too. The visits became occasional and then stopped.

Two years later I received a call from him to tell me that he was getting married. There were no heartbreaks, no complaints and obviously no explanations wanted or given. An invitation card followed. I attended the wedding and thirty years later, I attended his daughter's wedding too. How and from where he found my location and my phone number, I have no idea. But it was a pleasant surprise, when I found a card in my hand for his daughter's wedding.

A decade later I invited him to a bookshop where a book of mine was to be launched. The bookshop was not in my hometown but in the city where he had settled after retirement. He came. In the midst of a large crowd I met him. His hairline had receded to the middle of his head making his face look so different that, for a split second, I didn't recognise him! But then suddenly a wave of magic rushed in from somewhere and I found myself wrapped in ecstasy. He appeared impressed by the crowds which had come to hear about my book. I was impressed by his incredible magic wand, which had not lost its power to create a world of enchantment around me.

And today, after forty years and six, since I first met him, I still don't really know whether, that newcomer to the Academy, who swept me off my feet, ever shared my sentiments. But I know for sure that he respected them and handled them with care, the way no one else did. The way no one else could.

Real Sacrifice

Aslam's parents were very happy that Baqreed and so was his grandmother, Sharifun. They had a goat which they were going to sacrifice. All these years Aslam's family was the only one in the entire neighbourhood which was never able to buy a goat for Baqreed sacrifice, for goats were selling at a very high price. Every year the prices would go up enormously. Last year Aslam's father Fazlur Rehman had even gone to the goat market on three consecutive days, but had to come back empty handed to be tormented by his wife, Mehrun.

'Do you realise how embarrassed I feel when a share of meat comes from every home in the neighbourhood and I am never able to send them a return share?' Mehrun said in a complaining tone.

'I tried my best but couldn't get a goat within my means.' Her husband tried to explain.

'Nothing seems to be within your means, except getting up in the morning and going to your great office and coming late in the evening, after it is dark. If anyone else worked that hard he would have been a rich man by now,' Mehrun shouted.

Fazlur Rehman had had enough of her taunts, so he told her bluntly, "First let me tell you that Baqreed sacrifice is not to show off or to send return shares of meat to your neighbours or friends. And let me ask you a question, I know your father had made ample enquiries about me and my family and my salary and my post. Why then did he marry you off to me?'

'For the simple reason that you were a government servant and government employees don't just get their salaries, dry and simple, but much more over and above their salaries.'

Fazlur Rehman flared up. 'What do you mean by "much more over and above the salary," you shameless woman?' Then he called out to his mother, 'What sort of a wife have you tied me up with Amma? Her father, she says, married her to me because he thought I bring home a bribe along with my salary. I can't live with a woman who is so morally-deprived. Send her back to her father's house.' That reduced Mehrun to tears. But seven year old Aslam was happy. Not because his mother was shedding tears, but because his father couldn't bring home a goat. That meant that at least one goat was spared its life.

Fazlur Rehman's mother was a far cry from the typical mother- in-law, the stereotype. She was gentle and peace loving, 'Beta, what do you mean by "send her back to her father's house". Every family has different moral standards. She is your wife for eight years. You should have been able to convince her about your moral standards and converted her to those. I'm not going to drop her anywhere, she'll live right here.' After sometime, she went to her daughter-in-law and explained at length that the sacrifice of an animal becomes mandatory in Baqreed for one, who can spare money over and above his necessary expenses. One doesn't have to beg and borrow or, God forbid, take illegal money for buying an animal for the sacrifice. The matter ended there.

Sometime later Sharifun visited her daughter who was married in a well off family and lived in a nearby village. She had several cows and goats and many bighas of lands. She wanted to give a pair baby goats to her mother as a present.

'Look, my dear girl we live in a small house as you know. It is too small for us, human beings. Where will I lodge the two goats?' the mother said to her daughter, 'And goats dirty the place. I like a clean house.' But then she remembered the fight between Fazlur Rehman and his wife Mehrun and she immediately changed her mind and consented to accept the present of one of the two goats, the male one. She came back home and presented the goat to Mehrun, 'This is a present for you, now you look after it and bring it up.'

Mehrun was delighted. She took him in her arms, named him Moti and decided to bring him up with great care and love, so that he would be a fat and healthy one year old, by the time the next Baqreed approached. Everyone in the family bestowed a lot of love on him and were sure that his sacrifice next Baqreed would please Allah immensely. The family was not offering Him an animal they had bought with money, but one they had reared themselves and loved. Allah would surely shower them with blessings untold.

But in the midst of such joy Aslam was very sad. He was dreading the approach of Baqreed. As each day passed Aslam grew more restless and unhappy. Moti was his best friend. He would wait hours for Aslam to come back from school and would then start jumping with joy and running around him. Aslam too would never come empty-handed. On his way back from school he'd break a lot of tender leaves and stuff them in his bag, for Moti. How Moti loved to eat those leaves! That dear little goat! 'How can anyone think of killing him? How can Allah Miyan be pleased with someone who does such a cruel thing.' By now Aslam was eight years old but couldn't understand how the all merciful Allah Miyan could shower the cruel with blessings.

Time was ticking away faster than ever before. And now there were just three days left for Baqreed and Aslam had not yet been able to think of a plan to save Moti. 'If Moti is slaughtered I will die too. I will ask Abba to kill me,' Aslam told his friend Abbas in school.

'Your abba will never kill you. He loves you. All fathers love their children.' His friend replied.

'But my father told me that he loves Moti too and that is why he will slaughter him. Abba thinks that will make it a better offering in the eyes of Allah. Could that be true?'

'Must be true, my ammi and abba also say that if you sacrifice a goat which you have reared in your own home and you love him then Allah gives you more *sawab*,' Abbas replied.

"Amma told me that Allah Miyan loves everyone. Then he must love Moti also, how can he give *sawab* to anyone who kills him with a big knife?' And Aslam burst into sobs. 'Help me Abbas to save my Moti, you are such a good friend of mine.'

Abbas was so moved by his friend's tears, that he seriously set his mind to work. 'I will help you to save the goat but please don't cry,' he said.

'Quickly then, tell me how to save him, see I am not crying now,' Aslam pointed at his eyes, 'there are no tears in my eyes, they are both dry, see Abbas.' But he could not control the salty water waiting behind his eyes. As he spoke there was something that released a flood of tears again. And Aslam wept nonstop. Abbas, instead of finding a solution to his friend's problem, joined him in sobbing. Between his tears Abbas offered a suggestion, 'Aslam, my abba is very clever. I'll ask him to tell us how to save Moti.'

'But supposing he tells my abba? No, please. I may as well tell my own father.' Aslam was not in favour of taking any help from grownups. He knew that they would not understand.

'Abbas, keep it to yourself, don't tell anyone, I'll never be able to save my Moti's life if another person hears about my plans,' Aslam begged.

'O. K. I won't, but I will help you save his life. Whenever you need my help, call me.' Both friends parted on that note.

When he reached home his grandmother was alarmed to see his eyes. They looked red and swollen, 'Aslam, my dear child, you look as though you have been crying. What happened?'

'Nothing.'

Aslam's grandmother got up immediately and rushed to the child, pulled him close to her and asked, 'Did someone hit you, did someone say something nasty? Tell me my dear child. If anyone did so, I'll thrash him. My dear Aslam, please tell me.' His grandmother couldn't bear to see the little boy in tears. But Aslam didn't utter a word. He only wept. He made efforts not to cry but couldn't stop. His grandmother brought him a glass of cold water in his little copper glass. Aslam took it in his hand and threw it. That action brought his mother charging, from the kitchen, with a *chimta* in her hand, which she was all set to use on Aslam's back. Her mother-in-law pulled the instrument from her hand and said, 'Don't you dare raise your hand on the child. Can't you see he is in great pain; he is definitely facing some problem.'

'Why can't he tell us then? Who is stopping him? He has become very stubborn. Actually he has started spending too much time playing outside with the wrong children, No wonder he is getting spoilt.' Mehrun sounded angry.

'Dulhan, he's a child. He is not your age or mine. Children are shy to open up. I'll deal with him; you go back to the kitchen and do your work.' Mehrun's mother-in-law tried to cool her down. She then turned to Aslam, 'Unless you tell me what is troubling you, how can I help you beta. You know how much your daadi loves you, don't you?'

'Yes,' at last Aslam opened his mouth.

'Then tell me quickly, I won't let anyone know,' the old woman assured him.

'Let's go outside,' he suggested after thinking for some time. And both walked out into the open.

Aslam pulled his grandmother almost onto the road, stood there for several minutes, and then said, 'Daadi, I'm afraid you may not like what I'm going to say.' Aslam mumbled.

'So what, but I will definitely try to make things easy for you.' She said as gently as she could. Her voice gave him strength. 'Daadi, I don't want Moti to be slaughtered for Baqreed, I will not be able to bear it,' and he looked straight into her eyes, so appealingly, as though he was begging for mercy. Those innocent eyes, with that appeal for mercy shook the old woman's soul. She hugged her grandchild and wept. After sometime she wiped her eyes with her dupatta and said, 'Come, we'll sit on that bench.'

'Do you want to sit there and think whether you should help me,' Aslam asked hopefully.

'I am already convinced that I should help you, but yes, I do want to sit and think how to convince your abba and amma.'

Joy spread on Aslam's face and he got up and kissed his grandmother, 'Daadi you are fantastic!' he almost shouted with excitement.

'I must first explain to you what Baqreed sacrifice is all about. It is not just slaughtering an animal.' As she uttered these words doubt spread again on that tender face, wiping out the earlier layer of joy and hope. The grandmother didn't miss the change of expression on the child's face. 'No, no my child, I'll not go back on my word. I will tell you the story behind the Baqreed sacrifice, only if you are willing to hear.' The old woman's words lit her grandson's innocent face again with a ray of hope.

'Yes, Daadi I want to hear the real story.'

'Have you heard about Hazrat Ibrahim?'

'Yes I've have heard his name and know that he made the first sacrifice.' Aslam said, and looked at his grandmother expectantly.

'Today I will tell you why he sacrificed the sheep which came out of the bushes,' she said and then told him how Allah Miyan had appeared to Ibrahim in a dream and commanded him to sacrifice the thing he loved most; Ibrahim realised his son Ismail was the person he loved more than anyone else. Ismail too, was willing to lay down his life for the love of Allah. So Ibrahim and his son went into the deep jungle to perform the sacrifice because they knew that if they remained near their home, people around would not let the son be killed. Ibrahim did not want anything to detract him from his obedience to Allah.

There, in the forest, Ibrahim tied a cloth round his eyes so that his love for his son did not come in the way. And Ismail lay down before him to be sacrificed. As soon as Ibrahim put his knife over his son's neck, a sheep appeared from the bushes and Allah ordered Ibrahim to kill the sheep instead. 'Since then, in the name of Allah, Muslims all over the world have been sacrificing in Baqreed those animals whose flesh is Halal.' Sharifun completed the story and looked at Aslam for his reaction.

Aslam heard the story with interest. But he was still thinking of how to save Moti. 'Daadi, let's go home. Abba must be coming back from office. You have to convince him about Moti.' Sharifun realised that she would not be able to divert her grandson's mind. Both walked in. Sometime later Fazlur Rehman returned from office. Everyone sat down for dinner. Aslam hardly ate. He got up to wash his hands.

'You have hardly eaten beta. Are you alright?' Fazlur Rehman asked.

'I am feeling sleepy, Abba.' And he lay down on his cot and closed his eyes.

'Aslam doesn't seem to be well,' Fazlur Rehman remarked.

'I am worried because he was crying in the afternoon and was in a bad temper. Ask Amma, he was sitting with her for a long time.' Mehrun looked concerned. Both of them walked up to Sharifun, who told them what their son wanted. 'I think his problem deserves some attention from both of you,' Sharifun said.

'This is hardly a problem,' Mehrun said.

'She is right.' Fazlur Rehman endorsed.

'You may be right, children, but anything, no matter how insignificant, if it troubles a child to such an extent, it deserves to be given a thought,' Sharifun explained.

'But Amma, children don't take much time to forget. I am sure one day after the sacrifice he will forget about Moti. And will be playing around merrily.' Fazlur Rehman said.

'Exactly,' his wife agreed.

'Go to him anyway; give him a hearing, beta.' Sharifun advised.

And they went to the cot where Aslam was sleeping with his elbow across his eyes. The goat was sleeping near the cot on the floor. The father carried the parcel of new clothes he had bought for Aslam to wear on Baqreed.

'Aslam Beta, here are your Baqreed clothes, get up and see. You wanted to wear jeans and a top, didn't you? I have bought just that for you. Now get up.' Both the parents felt that he was awake. The mother gently removed his elbow from his eyes. His face was wet with tears. His mother lifted him up and clutched him close to her breast. 'What makes you cry my baby?' And Aslam broke into sobs almost hysterically. That upset the parents no end.

'Tomorrow I'll get you new shoes also.' Fazlur Rehman said.

'No Abba I won't wear new shoes and I won't wear new clothes either. How can I enjoy when my Moti will be killed so cruelly.'

'Moti will not be killed cruelly. He will be sacrificed. And he will go to Jannat straight away.'

'I want him here with me, not in Jannat. And I don't want that large knife to cut his poor throat. Oh Abba! Oh Amma! Spare him for Allah's sake!'

'It is for Allah's sake we'll be sacrificing him, giving him up, my child.'

'Give up something else, Amma, Abba, something you like, something you love. I'll give up eating sweets. I adore sweets. Once Amma gave me a plate of jalebis to take them to our neighbour when Abba's pay increased, I ate away two and gave the neighbour only the remaining. I'll never do that again. Amma, I'll press your feet every night, even if I'm very tired myself. Even yours Abba. I'll never play, I'll only study and help Amma in the kitchen.' Aslam was desperate.

Both the parents stood there, listened to their child's earnest words and wept. At last the father spoke 'Your Moti will live, dear child. Instead, I'll give up eating this deadly Pan

Masala, which takes away such a lot of our money and brings death closer to me.'

'And I'll never make efforts to appear richer than we are,' Mehrun said. And Daadi was not far behind. She quietly walked in and announced, 'From this moment my *paandan* is shut. Never again will I put any paan or tobacco in my mouth. And the money saved by giving up these bad habits will go to people who are poorer than us.'

Aslam's joy knew no bounds. He jumped from his cot and moved towards Moti to hug him. Moti had already walked to Aslam's parents and grandmother. He sat down there and started rubbing his mouth on their feet.

Panditayin

Nawab Ali Raza gave up hopes of fatherhood quite late in life, that is, when he was almost eighty years of age. He had no children though he married thrice. He was seventy-five when he married for the last time. He waited patiently for five years and then adopted his nephew's son. The nawab was the Taluqdar of a large area of land from which he collected a huge chunk of money. Then there was property too which he owned all over Hardoi. Actually he needn't have gone through the process of adoption, but he had no trust in the British laws, otherwise in the absence of his own children all his wealth and titles could have easily passed on to the next of kin, who was his nephew's son. There was one other problem. His brother and brother's son had passed away in the nawab's lifetime. So according to the Muslim Law his nephew's son had become *mahjub* and could not become the inheritor of his property and wealth, in the natural course. The nawab was therefore advised to make a will, giving his entire wealth to his grandnephew. He left no loopholes in the way of his grandnephew inheriting his entire wealth.

But the Almighty had planned otherwise. Nawab Ali Raza continued to live a healthy life till ninety. And at ninety he became the proud father of a bonny son. The girl he had married at seventy five was the mother. She was thirty three when she gave birth to the beautiful child.

Nawab Ali Raza was overjoyed. The first thing he did after offering thanksgiving namaz to Allah, was to call for the papers of adoption and the will. In the presence of high officials he cancelled them though he still gave a big chunk of land to his grandnephew. He was too happy perhaps to notice the disappointment on the faces of his younger brother's family members, but his young begum did and was terrified to see the rage and hatred which they could not hide.

'Nawab Sahib you should not have been in such a hurry to cancel the will and the adoption papers,' she gently addressed the nawab.

'Why?' he asked point blank.

'I don't think they were very happy about it.'

'Who are they?' he asked in anger.

'I don't mean to criticise anyone. But someone who was getting the whole amount would not be very happy with just a small slice,' the begum clarified.

'My brother and his family loved me. My grandnephew dotes on me, I am sure he would give up his life for me. This is not the time to criticise and find fault with others. Spend time on prayers to thank God. Get things ready for celebrations. I will not tolerate any aspersions cast on him.'

'I'm sorry to have hurt you. Please forgive me,' the begum sahib said and came back to her room. Immediately she called Panditayin, who had been her chambermaid ever since she came to the haveli as a young bride and was now the baby boy's nanny.

Panditayin came with the baby in her arms. 'Panditayin, my heart is full of fears. I don't know why but I feel something terrible is going to happen,' the begum said and started weeping inconsolably.

'Begum Sahiba, calm down, control yourself; what's the matter? Here, take your baby. What a lovely child Bhagwan has blessed you with. Put him close to your heart and you'll feel relieved.' While saying all that, Panditayin wondered why the Begum was in an unhappy state of mind. She had never seen her in that condition in all the fifteen years that she worked as her chambermaid. The begum took her baby and clutched him to her heart just as Panditayin had suggested, but a greater fear overpowered her. 'Mere Allah, what is it that you have in store for me? What is it that is troubling me, why can't anyone understand? Allah send someone to help me.'

Panditayin's heart reached out to her. She put her arms round her and said, 'I understand what is worrying you.' Begum Sahiba suddenly got up, placed the baby in Panditayin's arms and said, 'Panditayin, promise that you will protect this baby from all evil and bring him up as your own child, away from enemies, away from all dangers.'

'Yes Begum Sahiba, I will, I promise you I will. But you will always be there to supervise your faithful servant's work,' Panditayin was quick to reply.

'No,' Begum Sahiba screamed. 'That's no promise. Give me your word that you will be the real mother to him when I am not in this world. You will save him from his enemies then.'

Panditayin promised, tears rolling down her cheeks, without any further arguments. But she did enquire later as to what had happened when the begum sat behind the curtains watching the nawab and his grandnephew discussing matters with the officials of his court and with some English officials. The begum told the Panditayin everything and described how rage and hatred was bursting from the eyes of the grandnephew and his sons when the nawab was cancelling the adoption papers and the will. Her mistress's narration was enough for Panditayin to understand the reasons behind her fears. Theirs was a long relationship.

The begum was married only for two months when Panditayin's mother-in-law had brought her to the haveli for a full time job. The nawab's brother's wife was running the household then. She refused to employ her on the grounds that there were already too many maids on the rolls. Panditayin's mother-in-law did not give up. She approached the young begum who found it indeed surprising that the old woman had brought such a young girl for a twenty-four hour job.

'Begum Sahib, we have enough to eat but my son, that is her husband, died six months ago. She is a widow with no children. Bhagwan will bless you if you keep her in your house as your maid. She will bring her utensils and cook her own food. Nawab Sahib is a highly connected man, if she lives in his protection no one will dare to lift a finger at her. It has been hell for me to protect her from evil eyes.'

'Whose evil eyes?' the young begum asked.

'Everyone's, including my older son's, who is already married. And my husband agrees with him. He says, "A widow can expect no better life. At least we are not throwing her out. She will have a home." The old woman said that and looked at the begum for her reaction.

The begum thought for a minute and then said, 'Though I am the Nawab's Sahib's wife, I am new to this place and still very young. The lady who has refused to employ her is a very experienced person. I must consult my husband and take his permission, before I say yes.'

The husband gave his consent on the condition that the begum and the girl herself took the responsibility. 'Remember,' he also told the young widow in the presence of her mother-in-law, 'it is your responsibility also to protect your *izzat*.' The mother-in-law agreed.

'But why can't she share our meals?' The nawab queried.

'*Huzoor*, our caste and *dharam* will not allow that, we are *bees biswa* brahmins,' the old woman explained. The nawab left it at that.

The mother-in-law was told to come every day to see her daughter-in-law in the first week and then once a week for a month. If she was satisfied that the daughter-in-law was in safe hands, then she could leave her there for as long as she wanted.

It appeared the young widow was happy from day one and so was the mother-in-law. She brought her utensils and cooked her own food and attended to the begum. The young widow was called Panditayin by all and sundry. In course of time she became a sort of companion and friend of the young begum. The father-in-law and brother-in-law of the widow were also more than satisfied because they were getting the greater part of her wages.

Life was running smoothly for all of them. Particularly after the birth of the child, there was joy all around. 'What had suddenly perturbed the Begum to such an extent?' Panditayin was unable to understand, though the politics of the family was not unknown to her. Fatherhood which escaped the old nawab came to him when all hopes had crashed. She did understand that while it brought extreme happiness to him and his wife, it couldn't have brought joy to those who would have benefited if he had remained childless.

'Have a sip of water, my dear Begum Sahiba, and tell me what is it that you fear.' Panditayin said, offering a silver bowl full of cold water to the Begum.

'Don't ask me to spell it out. I don't want to utter those words with my tongue. I want my son to live long, a happy and healthy life. I don't mind if his enemies take away my life and all the wealth he is born with.'

Panditayin didn't want the begum to say anything more. She had come to love the child almost as much as his mother. She agreed totally that there could be evil schemes against the child. But what schemes? What strategy she should plan to defeat those schemes, she wondered all the time.

While Panditayin was planning out a strategy, the nawab had arranged for the *aqiqa* ceremony, a grand celebration for the first removal of the baby's hair. Relatives and friends had come from nearby villages to participate in the function. People were busy in the song and dance festivities till late night. The begum sat proudly with her baby, who had been named Hasan, in the midst of relatives. Panditayin sat a little away, but she was watchful. A woman who looked like a maid gently approached her and said 'You must be tired Begum Sahib, I'll hold the baby.' The begum got up, stretched her arms over those sitting around her and gave the baby, not to the woman who had offered to carry him, but to Panditayin, who took the baby, stood up and left the room. The woman followed Panditayin. The begum was surprised! She stopped her and asked her who she was. 'I am also your humble *kaneez*.' And she continued to pursue Panditayin. The begum walked behind the woman as fast as she could. At one point the woman took out a dagger and tried to stab Panditayin on her back. Luckily Begum Sahiba was still behind her, watching every move of hers. When she saw the woman take out the dagger from her clothes she gave her a push. The dagger clattered to the ground and Panditayin who knew every nook and corner of the haveli disappeared with the baby into some corridor and finally was out of the gate and then on the road, rushing towards her mother-in-law's house.

Panditayin and Begum Sahiba together had been successful in saving the baby. But carnage took place later that night in which the begum and the nawab both lost their lives. The loot and killings were made out to be the doings of thugs. Nawab Ali Raza's grandnephew became the next nawab. But he was restless. He knew that the rightful heir had not been killed in the carnage and so his position as nawab and taluqdar was not secure.

If the new nawab was restless, Panditayin could not be at peace either. Her in-laws were not willing to keep her in their house, more so with the baby. The news that the old nawab and his wife had been killed by thugs who had raided the place that night had reached Panditayin's in-laws' place. Like Panditayin they were also sure that the killings were not the doings of the thugs but that of the grandnephew.

'How can we keep you here? The new nawab knows that you and the baby are alive and that this is the first place where you will seek refuge.' Her father-in-law refused to give her sanctuary.

'How do they know that we are alive Bappa?' she gently asked her father-in-law from behind her *ghunghat*.

'The first thing they must have done was to look for your body and the child's and in the absence of the dead bodies they'll presume that you are alive, the boy is with you, and that you are here, in your late husband's home.' The father-in-law explained elaborately. This time the mother-in-law who was otherwise eager to give her shelter, also agreed.

'I understand, *Dulahin*, Bhagwan knows, the promise you have made to your dead mistress is sacred. I know you are bound by it. But you will have to think out some other place where you can take the baby and live in peace with him. We are poor people, we will not be able to protect you from those sharks,' the mother-in-law said.

'If you live here a day more you will have to part with the wealth the begum has given you,' this time it was her older brother-in law who intervened.

'I swear I had to leave suddenly, in the midst of all the celebrations, when a strange woman who had a dagger hidden in her clothes, tried to snatch the baby. Begum Sahiba had no time to give me any money or to prepare me for any exigencies. I just about escaped with the child. Please let me live here a few more days.'

'And who will explain from where the baby has come from?' And he pulled her by her arm and threw her out with her bag and the baby clutching on to her, while the rest of the family watched. 'That's what she deserves,' he said re-entering the house. But she got up and moved away before others from the neighbourhood could come from their houses to have a look at what was happening. And she continued to walk into the deep jungle. She did not fear the wild animals but she definitely wanted to be far from humans. She had intense faith in God and after she was thrown out of her husband's house she felt a kind of confidence developing in her. After sometime she saw that the jungle was thinning and a narrow road was meandering in the distance. And soon she found herself walking on the road. Directionless, but not aimless.

The child was both hungry and thirsty and crying nonstop. After some time, she stopped and looked around her. She saw some people walking behind her but at a sufficient distance. Her first instinct was to run into the jungle again and hide. She was sure they were sent to look for her by the new nawab. But her child was so hungry that she decided to stand behind a tree and wait. Maybe they were not the nawab's men but others from whom she could get some water for the child. As the procession of people passed the tree behind which she was hiding, she realised that none of the men were from the haveli where she worked. A woman who sat in a bullock cart looked familiar to her. She had seen her at the celebrations with a lady who had been invited and was throughout sitting with her Begum Sahiba. Suddenly she remembered that her Begum Sahiba's distant cousin who was also her very close friend and was married to the Zamindar of Baon had also come to the haveli to attend the *aqiqa* ceremony of Hasan, with her husband and little son. She became sure that this caravan was that of the Zamindar of Baon. She rushed out from behind the tree and reached the woman she had recognised and begged her for some water for the baby. Everyone in the bullock cart tried to help and fussed around the child.

When the baby was fed with some milk, Panditayin asked to be taken to the *zamindaarin's* palanquin. The *zamindaarin* was indeed the cousin of Panditayin's mistress who had told her of her fears much before the strange woman appeared and tried to take away the baby. Panditayin had escaped in her presence with the baby and of course she and her entire party were witness to the carnage. When the *zamindaarin sahiba* heard that she had no place to go, she and her husband offered to keep her with them. They told her that they were going to Lucknow and not to Baon.

'You can come with us to Lucknow. It would be a better place for you to stay and bring up this child. His enemies will search for him only in the vicinity. They will not have the faintest of idea that you or he could be in Lucknow,' the cousin's husband said. He was the Zamindar of Baon and a senior officer in the King's Army and now that his son was almost three he didn't want to keep him in the village. He wanted to give him a good education in Lucknow.

'Will I get an opportunity there to serve in a big house so that I could also educate my Hasan?' Panditayin asked. The Zamindar Sahib and his wife were very happy to hear those words from Panditayin's lips.

'Of course, Panditayin, I'll put in a word, in the King's household, for a job for you. Your Hasan will be ahead of everyone!' he said.

'Sugar and ghee in your mouth, Huzoor. May your words come true. May Bhagwan bless you,' Panditayin suddenly cheered up.

'But it appears nothing has gone inside your mouth for a long time,' the *zamindaarin sahiba* said and added, 'We have a Brahmin cook with us who cooks for our Ziledar, Raghubar Pandey and other Hindus travelling with us.' She asked the palanquin bearer to ask Raghubar Pandey to get some food for Panditayin.

Once in Lucknow, *Zamindaarin Sahiba* and her husband saw to it that Panditayin's need for shelter and all other requirements were looked after because they felt she was doing a noble job. Soon Zamindar Sahib arranged a good job for her, with a nobleman's wife.

Life moved on smoothly. Everything was fine so long as she called the child her own. It was dangerous to let out the truth about the boy's parentage because she was working among Lucknow's nobility, who were likely to know the boys' parents and his entire background. She could not afford to leak out a word about where she worked earlier or where she belonged. There was no problem in bringing up the child as her own because, she was in any case, promise-bound to bring up the child as she would her own. But the hitch was that the child's parents were Muslims and she found herself duty bound to bring him up as a true Muslim, despite the fact that that was not a part of the promise made to her mistress.

When he was old enough she put him under a Moulvi to learn the Quran. A time came when the boy himself asked why he had to read the Quran, when other Hindu boys were not reading it in the Madarsa.

'I want you to know more than others,' were the type of harmless answers she would give him and he'd be easily satisfied too. But as he grew older there were more questions to which he wanted answers and then the questions became endless. There came a time when she felt scared to answer his questions because one answer led to another question. And Panditayin felt he might reach the truth about his birth and if he did, a true answer would shock him. He had come to love her so much; the truth might fill his mind with doubts about her. He may even start hating her, God forbid!

She had sorted out some of his questions, for instance, the one concerning his religion. She told him that God had blessed her with a baby after she had prayed at a Sufi saint's Mazar. She had promised the saint that the child will grow up as a Muslim! This explanation was accepted without any doubts by the society too. The reality, she thought, could be revealed to the boy when he became older. But the reality about his parents and the great tragedy which surrounded their death, that was the real question. How was she going to tell him about that? Won't that cause a fit of rage within him? He would definitely want to know the perpetrators of the great tragedy and take revenge on them.

'And they will do away with him in minutes, he is all alone, a poor servant woman's son!' Panditayin said to herself. All she could do was to wait and let Hasan grow older. He was only ten and that was too young an age to face a revelation so ghastly. How was she going to disclose to Hasan the truth? How was she going to handle the situation? And the matter was put off when suddenly she saw two palanquins at her door with the *Zamindaarin Sahiba* in one and her son in another.

'Lock up your house, take whatever minimal luggage you need, take all your valuables and get into the palanquin with your son. Lucknow is not the place for us to stay anymore, at least not just now,' *Zamindaarin Sahiba* whispered in Panditayin's ears. Panditayin did as told because it was *Zamindaarin Sahiba* and her husband who had stood by her through thick and thin ever since they had met on the road on that fateful night. And then Panditayin saw a connection with the orders which the noble woman, her present mistress, had given her a few days ago. Panditayin was given a few months wages and told not to move out of her house. 'There is no need to come for work either,' she had said. Poor Panditayin had mistaken that as dismissal from work.

'Where is Zamindar Sahib?' Panditayin suddenly noticed that he was not there. 'I will tell you later,' *Zamindaarin Sahiba* said, in a whisper.

On Hardoi Road a bullock cart and two horsemen joined them. The horsemen were to guard the party on their way to the village. The bullock cart had some men who were to replace the palanquin bearers when they were tired. There were two cooks and a maid too. The horses were replaced several times when the party stopped at friends' houses in different villages. At last they reached Baon which was home of the *Zamindaarin Sahiba*. When they had settled down and had relaxed the two horsemen disclosed what they heard on the way. The King had been removed from his throne and Awadh had been annexed to the British Empire. The people in Lucknow were not safe. Panditayin recalled that Lucknow had looked eerie to her for quite some time. *Zamindaarin Sahiba* had been told by her husband, who was also a general in the King's Army, that there were plans for the King's Army to rebel against the British in the event of the annexation of Awadh. The mutiny had started. *Zamindaarin Sahiba* knew that her husband was leading the army. His life was obviously in danger. She spent most of her time praying for his safety. But it was not long, when a message was brought by horsemen from Lucknow that he was killed in action. *Zamindaarin Sahiba* and her twelve year old son were shattered. Panditayin did her best to help them recover from their great loss. *Zamindaarin Sahiba* realised, that till her son grew up, her lands were all that she could depend on.

Without any further waste of time she took a total stock of her lands. Each time the Ziledar would point out some land on paper she would tell Panditayin to take her son Abid and go out into the villages and check its actual existence. Soon she had a firm hold on her lands and no one could cheat her. And one day she told Abid, 'Though you have no dearth of lands I want you to be an educated man. I want you to study English also, I want you to earn my bread and yours by your pen.'

'I will study, Amma, as you tell me,' Abid replied.

Hasan who was standing nearby went to Panditayin, clung to her and said, 'Amma I will also be an educated man.'

'Yes my child, why not?' Panditayin said, love oozing out of every pore of her body.

'Amma I will also study English.'

'Yes my love, definitely,' Panditayin's joy knew no bounds.

'And since I have no lands I will have no option but to earn my bread and Amma's by the pen,' Hasan said this in jest.

'But in that case we will have to go back to Lucknow after taking leave from *Zamindaarin Sahiba,*' Panditayin said. And soon Panditayin and Hasan set out for Lucknow escorted by two of *Zamindaarin Sahiba's* loyal servants.

***

Lucknow had changed. But Panditayin managed to find her earlier mistress, who could no longer afford a maid, but referred her to many of the queens who did not accompany the king to Matiaburj. One of them employed her on a much higher salary than she had got earlier from the nobleman's wife. And that made Hasan's ambition to become 'educated' and study English possible. As he grew older he impressed many an Indian teacher who taught English and also one Englishman, who finally got him a job in which he rose quite early to the post of Inspector of Schools.

Panditayin was on the top of the world, but she still felt that the duty she had done towards him was not complete. He deserved to know his identity. Panditayin's mind started working overtime again.

'So what if he stops loving me, I'll bear that.'

'So what if he starts hating me, I'll bear that.'

'So what if he goes to those who had usurped his title and taken his property and fights with them and is killed – NO,NO NO,' Panditayin started screaming and crying as though in a delirium. Hasan came rushing in from the next room. 'What happened Amma, did you have a bad dream?'

'Yes,' she said and put off the matter till the next day.

But some day had to be the day; Panditayin was determined not to procrastinate anymore. And she didn't. The next day she made Hasan sit before her and told him the whole story. Hasan wept without control, like a child. He clung to Panditayin and said that he could not bear to think, for a second, that she was not his mother. 'I will not accept any Begum Sahiba as my mother.' He would repeat that and become hysterical. 'Why did you tell me this and spoil my life.'

At last Panditayin spoke. 'Has anything changed, my child, by my telling you this? Have I changed? I am your mother since you entered the world. And I will remain your mother not only till I die, but in every life. Birth after birth.'

'Never mention any Begum Sahiba or any Nawab Sahib or their wealth or their nephew, Amma,' Hasan begged.

'Never,' Panditayin assured.

'And we will live happily, just the two of us,' Hasan said.

'Just now, yes, just the two of us, but very soon, a third will also join, a bride, her face as radiant as the moon, then more and more will keep walking in and make a big happy circle,' Panditayin said. Hasan smiled and put his arms round her in a tight embrace.

Let Sleeping Dogs Lie

Atique was four years, four months and four days old when his parents celebrated his *Bismillah*, a ceremony which signifies the beginning of education in one's life. The proud parents wanted their son to be an educated man and the height of education for them was that their child should know the Quran by heart, so that he is respected in society and can go about with the prefix 'Hafiz' attached to his name; They were also convinced that the knowledge of the Quran strengthens the character of the individual, makes him honest, just and peace loving. They invited people even from their extended family and neighbourhood to watch him take his first lesson of the Holy Quran from a learned Maulana and thereafter to share with them a celebratory lunch. The parents also knew that all that a Hafiz could do was to teach the Quran but they never expected their son to accept money in return. They wanted him to teach the Quran to as many children as he could and spread the knowledge that is in the holy book without expecting anything in return. To earn a living they ensured that he acquired a skill. This was at the beginning of the forties of the 20th century. 1940 to be precise.

So the parents sent Atique, when he was some years older, as an apprentice of their friend who was an excellent shoemaker and also had a small factory of his own. Atique progressed well on both fronts. By the time he was sixteen he had completed the Holy Quran and in a few more years he had become a fairly good shoemaker too. Though he started earning his wages immediately after completing his apprenticeship, it took a very long time for him to establish a factory of his own. For years he had to work for others and be just satisfied with whatever wages were given to him for the day's work. And when he, finally, did own a factory he found it very difficult to supply the demand for his wares on time. Skilled and dedicated workers were not easy to find. They demanded higher wages, which he couldn't afford. How he wished in those days that his two younger brothers had also trained as shoemakers. They would have together run a factory and beaten all others in the trade. But by the time his brothers were old enough to begin their tryst with education, their parents had learnt about the importance of secular schools. The younger boys were put in Hindi schools though the parents gave them also the opportunity to learn the Quran as they had given Atique. The boys passed out from school with flying colours, but could not go to college. The parents couldn't afford it. At that time the government did not have too many schemes for meritorious students and there was not much awareness among the people about them. After completing their schooling, for years the brothers ran from pillar to post to get into government jobs, but all in vain. At last they learnt to drive four-wheelers and went away to Mumbai where they started driving taxis for a living.

Back in Lucknow the much respected Hafizji, by now Atique was addressed thus, had to slog for a decade and more for Lady Luck to smile on him. He almost reached middle age when a demand came from an exporter in Kanpur. Hafizji poured his heart and soul into his work, promised additional wages to his craftsmen, gave them an occasional lunch and several cups of tea during the day. He did just everything possible to keep their concentration focussed on their work. Hafizji knew that he couldn't take any chances with the consignment because the Kanpur exporter was to send the footwear to a very prestigious department store in London. His work would be rejected outright if a single flaw was detected. Hafizji's care and caution paid dividends. His first consignment was found flawless. And so were the others that followed. But for years, the payment he got in return from the exporter was paltry. And he got no credit for his work either. That hurt him most. It was the exporter's name which was embossed on the footwear. Hafizji was finding little time to work for the local market for all his concentration was focussed on the exporter's work. There were no financial gains, no encouragement and no inspiration whatsoever for him to pull on.

At last he decided to have a face to face talk with the exporter's manager. The manager expressed his helplessness. 'Hafizji, I understand your point of view and I have full sympathies with you, but I am only a paid employee. Why don't you meet the owner, the proprietor of the firm?'

'You arrange a meeting with him, Manager Sahib,' Hafizji said.

'Oh sure but you'll have to go to Delhi to meet him, he lives in Delhi.'

Hafizji had never been to Delhi, he had no arrangements for stay there. Coming to Kanpur was expensive enough.

'Manager Sahib, he has such a big business in Kanpur. He must be coming here sometime or the other. I am sure you will be good enough to arrange my meeting with him here in Kanpur,' Hafizji pleaded.

The manager got up, went to the calendar on the wall and stood there reading it. He appeared to be making some calculations. Then coming back to where Hafizji stood, he said, 'You are right Hafizji, he does come to Kanpur and you can meet him here. But that will not be before next year.'

Hafizji's face suddenly lost whatever life there was on it. He tried to say something, but couldn't. He found his throat parched. He sat down on a chair and asked for some water, which was brought by the manager himself. While giving him the glass of water, he said, 'Don't lose heart Hafizji, a year passes in a blink. How soon time passes, who would know that better than you?'

'I know,' Hafizji said. His voice was devoid of all expression as was his face. That expressionless voice and that blank face painted fear on the brow of the manager.

He suddenly got up, smote his forehead gently with his hand and said with mock concern, 'Hafizji, I'm really becoming forgetful. Obviously age is catching up with me. Kohli Sahib is going to Lucknow on Thursday. You won't even have to come to Kanpur. You can meet him in Lucknow. I will give you the address of the place where he will be staying.'

'Manager Sahib, kindly give it to me now, I have no telephone,' Hafizji said.

'But once you spoke to me on the telephone, I remember distinctly,' Manager Sahib reminded him.

'Yes, but I rang up from someone else's phone.'

'Hafizji, you're such a big manufacturer and you don't even have a phone!'

'I am a manufacturer alright, but a poor one and a poor one I will remain till I am given my rightful dues by those who buy my wares.'

The manager looked embarrassed and said he would try to get the address from the Proprietor's younger son who lived in Kanpur. Hafizji had to wait for some time but he did get the Lucknow address. The manager accompanied Hafizji till the door and said, 'I hope the meeting will be a successful one for you.'

Hafizji was no longer in a good mood. 'If payments are not made to me according to the fine quality of my footwear, I will stop supplying,' he said, his voice stern.

'Don't forget Hafizji, you've signed an agreement to work, till a particular period, for this Company. You'll have to supply your products till the period is over. Since you're not educated enough you may not have read the terms and conditions. I'm your friend, so I'm advising you, in your interest, don't lose your temper. Normally the Proprietor avoids speaking to uneducated manufacturers. He leaves them to me. I'll have to persuade him for this meeting. Actually he'll be doing you a great favour, please keep that in mind.' The manager said with a straight face.

Hafizji said nothing, quietly raised his hand in salutation and walked out. But he was fuming at the manager who so unabashedly called him, a person, who had learnt the Quran by heart and who had studied at the Nadwatul-Ulema, an internationally known University, uneducated. On the two and half hour train journey to Lucknow, he cursed himself for not having someone well versed in English with him when he was signing the agreement. He wondered how he could have signed a document, knowing that all that he could read was

Urdu and Arabic. Only later he had picked up some Hindi and a little English too. And that agreement was in English! He had learnt to write basic things like his name in that language, that's all. So he had signed the document in English! Otherwise he couldn't read the language, couldn't speak it, couldn't understand it. Nor did he know anyone who could. He had a copy of the agreement alright, but who would read it for him, he wondered. His children were still in school. They were very young. His daughter, the eldest among his children, was only in Class Eight, of a Hindi-medium school. If the Proprietor wanted to make a fool of him, he could very easily do it. It was in that unhappy and confused state of mind that Hafizji entered his house.

It was always his wife he turned to on occasions such as this. He called to her. She came rushing for she guessed that something was wrong. 'What is the matter? Is everything alright? You look worried.' And he told her everything, all about the agreement in English which he had signed. 'Who will read it now and explain it to me before I go to meet Kohli Sahib. The fellow can cheat me. From the way the manager behaved with me I doubt their intentions.'

'No one can cheat you; don't forget that there is Allah up there to protect you,' she said, pointing her hand towards the sky. 'Now come and have dinner, I've made your favourite dish. We'll discuss the matter after that. I'm sure we'll find a solution.' As Hafizji sat down for his evening meal, he noticed that the children were not around and asked for them.

'I am here Abba,' Razia called out from the kitchen where she was making chapattis for him.

'Here I am,' Ghufran said, putting a hot chapatti in his father's plate.

'And where is chote nawab, my dear little Rizwan?' asked Hafizji, forgetting, for a split second, the problem which was pestering him.

'He's asleep,' his mother said, but little Rizwan came rushing out from inside the room, 'No, I'm not, I am not. Abba what have you brought for me? Show me, come on, give me.'

'Let Abba finish his meal, he's hungry, he hasn't eaten the whole day.' The mother tried to calm the little one. But Hafizji got up, opened his bag, took out a box of sweets and handed it to Rizwan, saying, 'These are for all three of you and your amma.'

'Abba too,' the mother added. All five shared the sweets. And then little Rizwan went back to sleep. Razia and Ghufran came and sat next to their father on the takht after he had had his meal.

'Children both of you go and sleep now. Don't you have to go to school early in the morning?'Hafizji said.

'Yes Abba, we do have to go to school but we should also know what is troubling you.'

'No children, you are too young, I should not burden you with my problems.'

'I am no child. I am14, Abba,' Razia said.

'And I am 12,' Ghufran piped in.

Hafizji was desperate to share his problem with anyone who cared to listen. He felt so vulnerable. He found nothing wrong in opening up to his young children.

'You know children, I think the time has come for me to stop supplying my products to the Kanpur exporter. The price he pays me, for the products which I supply him and which have made his name famous internationally, is laughable. The high class craftsmanship which goes into the making of my footwear is rare. He's not likely to get it anywhere else in this region.'

'Abba, then why don't you stop doing his work? Tell him that you can no longer supply the goods at his price,' Razia suggested.

'Can he harm you if you stop supplying him the goods?' Ghufran wanted to know.

'Unfortunately I signed an agreement. I did not care to know the details of the agreement then, because I was too happy having got the chance to supply my goods to an exporter after years of supplying only to the local market. At that moment I didn't care. All that I thought of was the contract, which I got, for sending my goods to an international market. Besides, the whole document is in English of which language I know not much, at least I don't understand it. Supposing the contract was for more than the period that I have already worked?'

'Do you have a copy of that agreement?' asked Razia.

'I do have a copy, but there's no one I know who is a master of that language and who will go with me to help me plead my case. I don't have the money to hire a lawyer. I've already supplied the goods for five years to the exporter. The price which he has paid till now has remained the same.'

'Abba, allow me to read the agreement copy you have,' Razia said somewhat hesitatingly.

'My child, I know you're a bright girl but you're studying in a Hindi-medium school. You'll never be able to understand what's written in the document.'

'But let me try, Abba, please.' Razia begged.

Hafizji got up, went indoors and came back with some papers which he handed over to his daughter. The girl took some time to go through the document. And then, with determination, walked up to her father and spoke with utmost confidence, 'Abba, one thing I'm sure about is that Kohli Sahib had got this document signed by you only for a year. Obviously then you're no longer bound to this exporter anymore. Please don't worry, go to sleep peacefully.'

'You mean I signed on an agreement which was for just one year! And they kept me tied down to the firm, manufacturing shoes for them for four more years at the same price? I can't understand how they could have done such a thing.' Hafizji looked puzzled and angry.

'Don't underestimate your daughter or the teachers of the school you've put her in. English is taught in Hindi-medium schools also. Hafizji, it is time for you to sleep,' this time it was his wife who spoke.

'If Kohli could have fooled me for five years, it's all the more reason why I should not confront him alone. When I go to meet him on Thursday I should take someone who is sharper than him.' Hafizji was sure that Kohli and his manager would have prepared a bigger trap for him to walk into.

'Hafizji I've an idea. Can't you persuade your Vakeel Sahib to accompany you there,' his wife suggested.

'Which Vakeel Sahib?'Hafizji asked.

'Judge Obaidullah Sahib, who has given you space in his house, free of rent, for your factory.'

'What are you talking woman? Do you realise what a big name his is in his profession! He will go with me indeed! I can't utter a word in his presence. I feel so nervous. You'll faint if you hear what his fees is.' Hafizji chided his wife for speaking thoughtlessly.

'But you've often told me that he also works free for the poor, at times.' Hafizji's wife did not give up. 'And you also told me that he has a number of young lawyers who come to learn work from him. Perhaps you could persuade one of them to go with you after reading your document.' Hafizji did not lose his temper this time. But sat down on his bed for hours, without uttering a word and then retired for the night.

The following morning he went as always to the market to get raw material for the day's work and came back to his factory to allocate work to the waiting *karigars*. And then he proceeded to that part of the large house where Vakeel Sahib held his office and saw his munshi, his juniors and his clients. He stood in one corner of the room without a word, waiting for someone to notice him. Vakeel Sahib's munshi or his juniors may have noticed him but no one acknowledged his presence, or maybe no one dared to say anything in the presence of Vakeel Sahib. But when he got up to leave his chamber to get into his car, he glanced in Hafizji's direction and enquired about the purpose of his visit. Hafizji could only stammer the word 'Agreement' and stretch his right hand which held the paper towards Vakeel Sahib.

'Munshiji,' Vakeel Sahib called, 'Apparently Hafizji needs some help. Just listen to him. And ask Mathur to handle it.' Then turning to Hafizji, he said 'Don't worry, tell Munshiji and Mathur about your problem.'

Hafizji was overjoyed. After his meeting with Munshiji and the junior lawyer Mathur, he rushed home as fast as his legs could carry him. He wanted to give the good news to his wife and children. For once he forgot about his work. He appeared drunk with joy. 'Vakeel Sahib is not a man, he is an angel.. Are you listening?' He was talking to his wife.

'Yes I am. I always told you Vakeel Sahib was a good man.'

'Vakeel Sahib is sending his junior with me to Kohli. Razia, my child, where is she? You know, she was right. The agreement was only for a year. The manager and Kohli thought I'll never be able to supply them good work and they'll throw me out within a year.'

'Hafizji, first say Namaz for thanks-giving and then talk to me. I am also going to thank Allah for keeping us in the protection of such a good man.' Both husband and wife spread their prayer mats and offered their Namaz.

On Thursday which followed Hafizji went to meet the proprietor of the export firm to which he was supplying his goods, accompanied by Mr Mathur, Vakeel Sahib's junior. The proprietor did not meet them alone either. His Manager was with him. When the exporter wanted to know why he brought a 'stranger' with him, Hafizji replied, 'He is my lawyer, Mr Anand Narain Mathur, no stranger to me. Moreover your manager had told me that I am uneducated and that you do not like talking to uneducated people. It is for *your* convenience that I have brought him here.'

Kohli started the conversation on the presumption that Mathur was an inexperienced, less educated young man, but soon realised that he was not to be taken lightly. Neither Kohli, nor his manager had done their homework. They were now nervous. Mathur and Hafizji had come well prepared with all the facts of the case. When Kohli asked for some time, Mathur gave him a day's grace and said, 'We have made all the calculations fairly and squarely, with honesty. You owe us rupees five lakhs for all the consignments which you received from Hafizji in the last four years, payments for which should have been on revised prices. You can take a day to make whatever calculations you want. We won't accept a paisa less.' The alternative was a law suit for fraud and misrepresentation.

That made Kohli and his manager sit up and think. Sharp as they were, they soon realised that Hafiz Atique was not as defenceless or powerless as they thought he was. And when they realised that he had the protection of Justice Obaidullah who, after retirement, practised in the High Court and was a name to reckon with, they lost all the self-assurance and bluster they exhibited earlier. They offered to pay rupees four lakhs to Hafizji, begged him to forego one lakh and not to drag them in a legal case. On Justice Obaidullah's advice, Hafiz Atique accepted the amount. Even four lakhs was a lottery for him. In his wildest dreams he had not seen that amount.

Hafizji swore that he would never sign a document without understanding it and would work fearlessly but only for people who are willing to deal with him with honesty and integrity. With all that money in hand, he started making plans for educating his children in the best possible schools and colleges.

But conditions changed even before he could start weaving his dreams. The year 1992 ended with bad news and 1993 barged into his life and that of his family accompanied with tragedy. His brothers in Mumbai had by then slowly collected a fleet of twelve taxis and had also diversified their trade by entry into the food industry. One brother supervised while both the older sons of the two brothers sat at the food counter dishing out intensely popular Lucknavi cuisine. The brothers had managed to hire some space near Null Bazaar very close to the Gole Deval which they called 'Lucknow Dastarkhwan.' People came from long distances to sample their Galawati Kababs and Yakhni Pulao.

The older brother had one more son for whom he was now setting up a furniture business in the same area. To begin with, they decided only to manufacture on demand. To hire a showroom was not easy. The manufacturing space which they managed to get was also in the same area. Mumbai had indeed been lucky for the brothers. Hafizji visited them for the first time, with his family, after his success with the exporter. He couldn't afford to take a holiday earlier. He was indeed happy to see them living in such affluence. He had heard their success stories earlier from his parents who lived part of the year with them and came back to live with him for the rest of the year.

But money is like a rolling stone and so is luck and happiness. In 1992 hatred stormed into their part of the city and shattered whatever they had built with their hard work and sacrifice. The timber stored and the ready-built furniture was put on fire which spread to neighbouring buildings and to their food counter where destruction multiplied because of the bursting of the many gas cylinders. There was loot in the garage too where their taxis were parked. They were left with just two taxis which had been hired a day earlier for a wedding party which was on its way to Bhusawal. One of the brothers and his nephew, who were driving them, were spared the horrific scenes of murder and arson in Mumbai where people were killed like flies. There was no one to save them. Even policemen went around brandishing naked swords. And yet fortunately no one from the two brothers' families, who were in the midst of the mindless butchery, lost their lives.

'This was by the grace of God. He will never cease to perform miracles. He will help you all to resettle, have faith in Him.' This was how Hafizji addressed his younger brothers when both prodigals came back to Lucknow, with their families. But everyone knew, as did Hafizji, that the road to settling down again did not pass through the Milky Way. It was long and arduous.

Hafizji and his wife did all they could to make the lives of their brothers and their children comfortable but they were in a state of extreme shock and trauma. They had witnessed devilish scenes which they found difficult to erase from their minds. Adjustment also became a problem, for the children particularly, who were born and brought up in Mumbai. For them to adapt to Lucknow of the 90s was not easy, though the two brothers wasted no time in getting back to the only work they could do. That was driving. But taxis were hardly used till then within Lucknow. They could earn something when they were hired to go out of the city or when foreign tourists wanted to see the city. The younger children were put in school but the three older sons could not even drive the taxis, for short periods, to give their fathers some rest, for they did not know the city. They longed to go back to Mumbai. They thought they could still salvage some of their belongings. Maybe their food counter! They could start it again if their old cooks were still around. But their parents and Hafizji were adamant not to let them go. And just as well they didn't.

Peace was unable to find its way back to Mumbai. Hatred was lurking in the wings, waiting for a cue to raise its head again. And come March 1993, *Bomb Blasts* flooded the streets of that great city again with the blood of its citizens. This time even the young sons of the two brothers gave up the idea of going back to Mumbai. They started looking around for possibilities of finding work in Lucknow. And soon they did. They started selling biryani outside Hafizji's house because to hire commercial space was not easy.

'We are so sorry, Barre Abba, to be messing up your doorstep,' Mansoor, his nephew, said, to Hafizji.

'Never mind, never mind, this is your house too. And, with the hard work you are putting in, I'm sure you both will soon become owners of a Hotel Insha-allah.'

'Barre Abba, we may also get compensation for all that we lost in Mumbai, our *Hotel* may come up earlier!' Hafizji's younger nephew, Arif, said with joy.

'What is this compensation you are talking about?' Hafizji asked.

'You know, the government has ordered an inquiry and set up a committee headed by a very honest judge who is bound to give a genuine report of the findings. These two boys think, that when he gives his report, the culprits will be punished and those who suffered at their hands will be given compensation.' Hafizji's younger brother, who was cleaning his taxi parked on one side of the road, explained. Both the brothers laughed so loudly that the third one also came out of the house.

'What are you two laughing at?' he asked.

'At how naive young people can be!' Hafizji's younger brother, who was cleaning his taxi, said.

Hafizji thought that it was the best time to give the young people some sound advice and added, 'Dear children, depend only on your own hard work. Don't wait for any compensation. Keep on struggling. There will be many more ups and downs in your life and in the lives of your dear ones. Stay together. Keep the family together. That will be your only strength. The honest judge can only write a truthful report. Those who take action on the report are others.'

'But why won't the *others* take action on the truthful report?'

'Because some truths are embarrassing,' Hafizji said with finality and went into the house.

Life moved on, while Hafizji and his two brothers lived with their children in this world. And life moved on even after their exit. There were *Ups*, like when Razia became a dentist and Ghufran and his two cousins became engineers and got good jobs. And also when Mansoor and Arif with their younger cousin Rizwan became owners of a most sought after eatery which had several branches in Lucknow. And *Downs*! It was a terrible *Down* when Razia's husband, an associate Professor, was arrested in a case of bomb blast. And *Ups* again, when he was let off after twelve solid years, for lack of evidence. And all those twelve years the family continued to fight together for the truth. They knew he was innocent.

***

Q. And what happened to the inquiry which the honest judge was conducting in the Mumbai case?

A. Yes he brought out a Report five years after he was appointed and a thoroughly frank and truthful report it was.

Q. Then did the boys get their compensation?

A. Which boys?

Q. Hafizji's nephews.

A. You mean the two old men who run the famous eateries?

Q. Yes, maybe.

A. But what compensation?

Q. Didn't the findings of the 'Truthful Report' get them compensation?

A. But the 'Truthful Report' was never read. And today, the fact is that the 'Truthful Report' requires specially designed spades to remove the dust which has accumulated on it in the last twenty odd years. Now since the old men are also not bothered, perhaps because they see themselves too, under tons of dust in the near future, they don't want to disturb sleeping dogs, they prefer to let them lie!